Seventh Mark - Part 2

Hidden Secrets Saga, Volume 1

W.J. May

Published by Dark Shadow Publishing, 2013.

Seventh Mark

Hidden Secrets Saga
Part 2 of
Book I
By
W. J. May

Book 3 coming summer 2014

Hidden Secrets Saga:
Download Seventh Mark part 1 For FREE
Book Trailer:
http://www.youtube.com/watch?v=Y-_vVYC1gvo
Website: http://www.wanitamay.yolasite.com
Facebook: Author-WJ-May-FAN-PAGE
Cover design by: Book Cover by Design
Edits by: Regina Mitchell
Book III – *Marked by Destiny* - Coming 2014

Also by W.J. May

Hidden Secrets Saga
Seventh Mark - Part 1
Seventh Mark - Part 2

The Chronicles of Kerrigan
Rae of Hope
Dark Nebula
House of Cards

The Hidden Secrets Saga
Seventh Mark (part 1 & 2)

The Senseless Series
Radium Halos
Radium Halos - Part 2

Standalone
Shadow of Doubt (Part 1 & 2)
Five Shades of Fantasy
Glow - A Young Adult Fantasy Sampler

Acknowledgments

To everyone who loves to read, thanks for letting words come to life!

Chapter 1

Caleb tapped his thumb impatiently against his other hand. A scowl etched his face as he sat behind a newly replaced, antique desk. "What's so important you had to come back to *my* house, Rouge?"

Settling by the fireplace, I tried to remember to breathe. He was intimidating as a person, but freakin' scary as some kind of immortal killing machine. *They must know Damon's a Grollic. How could they not?* I swallowed, not as sure of myself as I had been moments earlier. "H-Have you been able to find anything out about D-Damon?"

"Very little actually," Sarah answered. "It's as if he is nothing, but we know there's something. He's seventeen, born here, lives here but nothing to raise concern to us."

Grace stood by the door frame. She had nodded when she had come into the living room but had avoided making eye contact with me. Now she stepped forward, uncrossing her arms. "There's no proof on anything. He's just...Damon."

Show them. A voice inside of me spoke, strong and determined. I set the old, leather journal in front of Caleb, my eyes defiantly meeting his. Where'd this new courage come from?

He picked it up, frowned at the cover and then flipped it open. I cleared my throat. "Damon's a Grollic. It was him at the beach. He has the beasts tattoo below his right collar bone." I turned to Grace. "That day in the courtyard, I saw it. Didn't realize till this morning what is was. I read through the book last night, and then remembered it this morning."

"What mark? They've no tattoo to label them." Caleb slammed the journal on top of the desk with a resounding slap. "Where'd you get this?"

His accusation really said was, *Where'd you steal this?* "It's from the bookstore where I work. My boss gave it to me." I tried to swallow, my mouth suddenly dry.

He traced the cover and bindings. "This book appears written over hundreds of years ago. The writing's in some ancient language." He flipped though the pages. "I've never seen or heard of this. The Coven doesn't know."

Lucky me. "Most of it's foreign," I mumbled, playing with the Siorghra around my neck. "I read through the part I could understand. Where it shows the anatomy of the Grollic, it talks about how he transforms even some theories on ways to kill him. The book's old, but you might be able to use something. There's a story about a girl in a white cape. I think she was an angel."

Caleb gasped and stared at me, his eyes blue and pupils tiny. Sarah and Michael raced behind him and hovered over his shoulder. Caleb gave his head a slight shake and focused back on the book. He held it at arm's length, probably so Michael and Sarah could read it.

Grace ran over and looked ready to hug me but held back. "You've no idea how much I've missed you," she whispered, her voice breaking.

"Me, too." *So why didn't you come by?* I paused, mad at my next thought. *Why didn't I try to text or email or come here sooner?*

"Oh Grace. Put those trivial female feelings aside. Now is not the time. Rouge should have shown us this book the moment she had it." Caleb turned me. "How long have you had it?" He shook his head. "Never mind. What I want to know is when did you learn the language?"

What? A heavy feeling dropped into the pit of my stomach. "I didn't. I can only read the English part." Did I need to show them? The book wasn't that big. Surely they could find the section.

Michael stared at me, his mouth slightly open. "None of the book's in English."

Supernatural immortals and they can't tell the difference between English and foreign? "The middle part is. It's like the Little Red Riding Hood Nursery. The part with the diagrams and drawings is where I connected the dots. That's where I found Damon's tattoo or mark or whatever you want to call it."

"I do not understand," Caleb spoke slowly. "Show me the part you can read."

This was ridiculous. Here I stood trying to help them and they are talking to me like I'm the idiot? Jaw clenched, I stomped over to the desk and grabbed the book. Searching through the pages, I found what I needed and tapped the title. "See, here. The History of the War. It's just like the fairytale, except Riding Hood's actually some kind of angel or something – she's got wings – and the Grollic's actually an ugly beast." I watched the three of them standing around the desk. Sarah had her hand against her chest, Caleb's lips pressed into a thin line, and Michael kept looking at me, then the book and back again.

"Rouge," he spoke slowly, "it's not English."

"What?" I shook my head, glancing toward the ceiling. "You're not funny."

"I'm not kidding." His face stayed serious, not a glimmer of teasing in his eyes or a twitch around his lips like he was trying to hold laughter in.

"Check this page." I pointed to the paragraph about Grollics' knowledge on the woman in the white cape. "The book's old, but the author wrote what they thought was a race from an original. He knew they could destroy you. See the list?" I flipped to the next page. "Here's the diagram of the Grollic and where its heart is located. The caption says that instead of being on the left side of the body, the Grollic's heart is on the right, located higher than most animals. The bit beneath the drawing, says when the Grollic changes from human to Grollic-form, the heart shifts. I guess if a human wanted to stab a Grollic to kill it, you'd need to aim for the right, not the left side."

No one said a word. Not even Caleb. His mouth actually hung open now.

What the –? "Listen. I can't read the beginning or the end of the book, but the middle section's in plain English..." Why only to me? I tossed the book on the desk, and rubbed my eyes, frustration giving way to confusion. "I don't understand. None of you can read it?" Grace came around, sat on the top of the desk and began flipping through the pages. The look on Michael's face confirmed the answer to my question.

He walked over and took my hand in both of his. He turned to Caleb. "What do you think?"

"I'm at a loss, but I intend to find out. This girl is no Grollic, and for everything we know, I've never had knowledge of the marking. This could be radical, for all of us." Caleb looked at me but avoided making eye contact. "The Coven meets tonight. With your permission, I'd like to take the journal along. If there is anyone else who is able to decipher the writings, it could be of key importance in bringing the mongrels into extinction." Caleb tapped his perfectly manicured fingernails on the desk.

The book belongs to me now. I shook my head. *What a weird thought.* "You don't need my permission. Take it. Keep it."

"No. It's yours." Caleb shot a glare at Grace who looked like she was about to say something, but closed her mouth. "I think you should take Rouge into my office and show her some of our history. See if there's anything else she's able to understand." He clicked his tongue and stood. Walking over to me, he pulled at my hood and touched my collar bone with ice cold hands that instantly turned warm. "No marking, 'eh? Just checking." A hoarse laugh came from deep in his throat, like he didn't do it often. "I'm interested in this little talent she's acquired."

A muffled growl filled the room. Everyone flinched and turned to me. I held my hands in the air. "That was my stomach."

Grace burst out laughing. She jumped off the desk. "Let's get you something to eat. We'll stop by your place after and grab some clothes." She glanced at Caleb. "We'll be working late tonight, so Rouge's going to need to sleep over."

"She needs to stay here. It's not safe for her to be on her own," Michael said. "I'll take her."

Grace put her arm around my shoulders and poked Michael. "You have to go with Caleb; you're expected to be there. The elders will be upset if you're not."

Michael, about to argue, must have changed his mind. "Fine."

Was there some hierarchy line? Where did Michael stand? If Caleb was royalty, would that make Michael some kind of prince?

"If you're able to find anything out," Michael said, "contact me and I'll come back. Now I'm going to talk to Rouge. Alone." He stared at Grace, and tapped the side of his temple.

Without waiting for an answer, he took my hand and led me out to the backyard. The feel of his hand in mine brought little electrical currents throughout my entire arm. He could have led me into a pit of Grollics and I'd have followed in a heartbeat.

Every piece of greenery in the back looked immaculately cut, set around a pool and a cute pool house. Barely had Michael shut the door when he pulled me into his arms. He held me tight against him. "I'm so sorry. Please forgive me."

I kissed him. Whatever disappointment, anger or heartbreak I felt had disappeared the moment he'd grabbed my hand.

He groaned, and one of his hands came up to my neck. His fingers drummed along my neckline to the pendant of his Siorghra. I could feel him smile through our kiss, and suddenly his kissing became more intense. I went right along with him, my hands running through his hair, on his neck, his face, on his chest. I couldn't get enough. I wanted more. Being apart had been harder than I realized.

He pulled back, his stunning blue eyes flitting back and forth to mine.

I gently leaned toward him, letting my forehead touch his.

"I'm so sorry," His voice cracked. "I blamed myself and thought I'd put you in danger and messed your world up. You were meant to find us. I should have known. I really missed you and I'm sorry."

I took a small step back and brushed a fallen hair from his forehead. "Don't be. Things happened for a reason. I'd have never looked through the book if I wasn't on my own."

He shrugged, not looking completely convinced.

My arms wrapped around his waist and I pulled him into a hug. I ran my palms along his back and froze when I came across his bony shoulder blades. I thought back to the journal.

"What's wrong?" he said, leaning back.

"Do you have wings?"

He chuckled. "No. There are a lot of things I can do, but flying is not one of them."

I reached for his shoulder blades again, remembering before the Halloween party when I'd first noticed their boniness. "But..."

"We all have those protruding little bits, maybe a leftover part that never evolved with time." He scratched his head. "I could have had them before...everything changed. I just don't remember."

"Oh," I blinked. "Wait a sec." What else had he just said? "What other things can you do?"

"Loads of cool stuff." He smiled. "I've been trained to fight. And when one doesn't have the fear of dying, it lets you push your limits a lot further. You learn a lot about the body's ability. "

"Can you teach me?"

Michael stepped back, apparently mortified. "No! It'd kill you."

Shaking my head, I playfully punched him in the arm. "I meant to fight. If I'm going to be hanging out with a bunch of people who hate Grollics, I should know how to defend or at least protect myself."

"Now that might be a good idea." Squatting, he reached for my arm and pulled me over his shoulder. "I think you're lighter than a sack of potatoes."

"Put me down." I pounded his back lightly. "I don't mean now. You need to go with Caleb, and I don't want to start any problems when I might have just scored some points with my crazy Grollic reading ability."

Michael set me down and smiled. "I love you." He tapped his Siorghra pendant. "You've already got my heart."

I blinked and straightened. No one had ever said those three words to me. Not the mother who'd abandoned me as a baby, the father I had no idea of, the foster parents I'd had through the years, or any guy I'd gone on a few dates with. Not even a best friend. *Is it possible to be terrified and ecstatic at the same time?* I ran my teeth across my lower lip. If I said the words back would something inside me change...forever?

"Probably should have kept that too myself." He chuckled and kissed my nose. "I think it's a good idea we go back in, you need to eat. You look a bit faint." He led me to the back door, through the kitchen, and into the living room. "Grace, can you take Rouge to get some food?"

I realized that while we were outside, I'd never bothered to pay much attention to what the backyard looked like, I'd been too busy concentrating on the hot body smothered against me. My skin grew warm at the thought.

Michael squeezed my hand and then darted into Caleb's office. I stared hungrily at him for a moment and then turned to Grace.

She burst out laughing. "You might want to put your ponytail back in, your hair's a mess."

Face burning, I reached for my hair and tried to tuck the escaped wisps behind my ears.

Grace didn't say another word, but her giggling didn't stop the entire drive to Jim and Sally's.

We walked through the front door of the house.

"It's so quiet. Are the foster-folks out?" Grace held her arm out to stop me. She cocked her head to the side. "This normal?" she whispered.

I sucked in a quick breathe, instantly paranoid. "Maybe. I ran out earlier today without talking to them." I glanced around. "Nothing seems out of the ordinary."

"You wait here by the door. I'm just going to have a quick look around to be sure." Grace darted away before I could argue.

I leaned back against the doorframe and checked up and down the street. Nothing was different. Hopefully Jim and Sally were out. Besides being freaked out by Grace tiptoeing thought the house, Jim had been freaky-weird the last time she came inside. I didn't want to have to deal with that again. When she walked back from the kitchen I said, "Let's go upstairs so I can have a quick shower, and grab clothes for tomorrow."

"First let me make sure everything's clear upstairs." She took the stairs two at a time.

I followed once she hit the landing. By the time I reached the top, she'd checked the rooms and turned back to my room. "How about you stay the weekend? You shower and I'll have a look through..." She paused, as if searching for the right word. "I'll check what's in your closet and see if there's anything I can do something with." A hand flew to her mouth. "I don't mean that in a bad way. I just meant..."

I laughed. I'd miss her being around. "I've got a duffel bag on the closet floor. You can throw what I'll need in there."

Opening the bedroom door, I saw why Grace had paused. My room had shoes and piles still on the floor from my lame attempt at sorting it last night. "It's not always this bad." The argument sounded really lame and Grace's raised eyebrows stopped me from bothering to say more. Instead, I grabbed a pair of jeans and the pretty, silver top Grace had bought before heading into the bathroom. The water needed to run for like an hour before it would heat up enough to step in. Stripping down, I stepped into the shower. I reached into my toiletry bag and grabbed a razor and shaving cream. Always better to be safe than sorry.

My shower lasted longer than my usual ten minute one. A twinge of guilt reminded me I'd made Grace wait. I dabbed a little perfume on, then grabbed my hair dryer and headed back to the bedroom. I didn't see her right away, but I did see clothes flying out of my closet with lots of muttering going on inside of it.

She came in and out of the closet, throwing assorted bits of clothing into the suitcase. The closet was one of those old ones, kind of square shaped with hangers set on the side, perpendicular to the door. As I towel dried my hair, she continued to come in and out with more clothes. Even my dresser drawers had been opened. She rolled three pairs of my jeans and then stuffed them into the near overflowing duffel.

"Whoa. I'm only staying the weekend. That's a lot of stuff."

Grace shot me a sympathetic smile. "I think I got everything that can be salvaged from your closet and dresser. While you were showering, Jim came back. He was on the phone and now he's downstairs in the living room. It sounds like he wants to talk to you."

"How'd you..." I didn't finish the sentence. She obviously had some super-sonic hearing or something. "You're joking? Of all nights." I stuffed my hair into a bun.

"He seems pretty fired up."

"What did he say on the phone?" *What am I? An eavesdropping ten year old?*

"He was talking to Sally. They were fighting."

"On the phone? That's weird. Guess I'd better go see." I was reluctant. Dealing with Sally had always been a two way street, with Jim it felt more like a one-way with bad construction.

I walked down the stairs and found Jim pacing in the living room.

"Hey. What's up?"

Jim muttered something under his breath.

All I caught was the word, "disrespectful." The sharp intake of Grace's breath told me she'd followed me down the stairs and had heard than I did. Jim's head shot up when he heard Grace. He gave her a weird smile, then he turned to me.

"Where's Sally?" I asked before he had a chance to speak.

"Gone. Flew back to Ontario." He took a swig from the liquor bottle I hadn't noticed before.

"What?" The word was out before I could stop myself. *She left, and didn't say good-bye? Surely not.* "Everything okay in Niagara Falls?" Maybe something had happened to hear family.

Jim snorted. "Figures you'd take her side." He pointed an accusing finger at me. "You think it's all a joke. You and her have probably been laughing at me not finding a job."

Huh? "I—"

"Don't bother. I can see it in your eyes." He began pacing the room. "You know what? You're out. I want you out. Sally was the one who wanted to help your hopeless ass, I only agreed for the crap money. You're eighteen next month and I'd have booted you out then. Why wait?"

Who would throw a girl with no family out on the street? "I've got no where to go!" Sally must have left him. Left us. We weren't super close, but still. What would make her just up and leave? Unless *something* had scared her.

Grace stepped in front of Jim, inches from his face.

I blinked. *Did she somehow make herself look taller?*

Grace spoke quietly but the power behind her voice made me glad she was on my side. "This place is a dump. You should be shot for the care you've offered. I've seen scum in this world, and you appear to be on the lowest rung. Rouge deserves better than this."

Startled, Jim shot her a nasty glare. "Shut up!"

Grace didn't bat an eye. "I never met Sally, but I'm not surprised she left." She laughed a sound between disbelief and sarcasm. As she stepped back, she grabbed the duffle bag. "You've been such an example for Rouge—"

"Of course we have," he snapped.

"—on what not to do in life," Grace finished.

"Get out! Both of you and don't ever come back, Rouge. Ever!" Jim hollered.

Grace pushed me toward the door to the fresh air outside, and led me to the passenger seat. She threw the bag into the back of the car.

"Stay here. I'll double check if there's anything else in your room you're going to need."

I sat in the car, too dumbfounded to respond.

Life freakin' sucked. I was officially screwed. Being able to read a weird language as if English and kicked out of the only place I was barely able to call home. *What do I do?* I leaned my head back onto the seat and closed my eyes. *Where was I going to go?*

Chapter 2

Grace jumped into the driver's seat and tossed my iPod, along with a roll of hundred dollar bills wrapped in elastic into my lap. She set my laptop on the backseat. "You deserve your last government check. That's all the cash he had on him. I should send Caleb back next week for the rest."

I stared at the cash, then unrolled it and counted. *Eight hundred dollars.* Folding them, I aligned the corners and then stuffed them into my jeans pocket. My mouth didn't know how to move and my brain couldn't get out of its fog of disbelief.

"Don't worry." Grace patted my forearm. "Everything's going to be fine." She squeezed the bridge of her nose with her fingers. "You need a place. You can stay with me in my room, but you're going to want privacy. With our abilities, you'll never feel like you were on your own." She sat in silence, glaring at the front door then straightened. "I got it! I'll talk to Sarah first, but I know she's going to say yes."

"Uh, what're you talking about?" I sat watching the windows fog, unsure of what to do and scared to think.

"We have a pool house in the back. Sarah had it built last summer in case... in case we invited school mates over and didn't want to worry about Caleb. It's not huge, but there's a big room with a futon, and it has a bath and a bar that could be used as a kitchen." She nodded as she started the car. "Yeah, it'll work out perfectly."

"I can't stay at your place." Caleb, if he were still alive, would probably have a coronary. *However, being that close to Michael...* I shook my head to clear my thoughts.

"Put your pride away. Be realistic. You've got no where and we have space. We can't – I won't let you go back to Niagara Falls. You're my best bud."

"Thanks. I'm just not sure what to do." I rubbed my temple. Had I told her I used to live in Niagara Falls? "Maybe for a few days I'll stay. Then get myself sorted."

Grace sighed. "Rouge, you're involved in this – in us - whether you want to be or not. We're not leaving you. I made that mistake last time, now I'm making up for it."

The house in front of me began to blur. I wiped the tears away with the back of my hand. Grace wanted to look after me. No one in my entire life had ever stepped up for me. She'd put Jim in his place, and now planned out where I'd rest my head. "Th-Thanks."

She smiled and reversed the car. "Think nothing of it. Be glad I came instead of Michael. Things would've been flying then." She laughed. "He can be a bit like Caleb sometimes." She shifted into drive and tore away from the house. "Don't worry about sleeping arrangements. We need to go home and get you into Caleb's office. Maybe you can find where the Grollics went. Seems all the beasts go into hiding or running when Caleb comes around." Grace danced in her seat. "I can't wait till Monday. I want a camera to take a picture of Damon's face when we walk in together."

I chuckled, the tears drying up. *Great, now I'm relying on dead people to keep me safe and entertain me.* Something was wrong with this picture.

Grace tilted her head and inhaled. "What are you wearing?" She sniffed the air, her little nose scrunched up and her lips puckered. "You always smell like licorice, but now I smell something different."

I started laughing. "I smell like licorice? Not sure if that's a compliment. I'm not wearing anything different. I just showered." Then I remembered putting perfume on. I hardly ever wore it, but did it on a whim. Suddenly my fingernails needed a good picking. I debated leaving it at that, but knew better than to lie to her nose. *Get ready to be teased for trying to smell pretty around her brother.* I mumbled, "I'm wearing a bit of perfume."

"Hmmm... it's nice. What is it?"

"Eternity." My head popped up, instant burn hit my cheeks. *They're immortal and this little human looks like she's trying to be around forever. Great, and now I'm talking in my head in third person.* "I honestly...I didn't...do it on purp—"

"Sure." Sarcasm dripped from her voice. She did her one eyebrow raise, same as Michael's, and we burst out laughing. We couldn't stop. Each time we calmed down, we'd look at each other and start all over again.

Pulling into their driveway, we finally sobered. I swallowed my gut muscles hurt like crazy. "Seriously though, I hope I'm able to help. I still don't get how the Grollic book isn't in English."

"Total freaky, but so awesomely cool. Bet you wish you could do the same with calculus." She giggled. "We'll go through some old books of Caleb's. You need to understand our history, not just the opinion of some Grollics on what started the war. You being able to read part of that book is invaluable to us. He'll be bringing it to the elders of the Coven—you're going to be famous in our world. The mortal who could read Grollic."

We walked into the house, having to drag my meagre belongings due to being weak with laughter.

Sarah met us in the hall wearing an apron and a smile. "I'm cooking dinner. It's going to be about an hour."

"Th-Thanks," I stuttered, suddenly very conscious of how homeless I actually was.

"Has Grace been rubbing off on you?" She pointed to the bags. "First time you stayed here, I thought you only had a backpack."

"She got booted out of her house." Grace put her arm around my shoulders. "Her foster parents are losers. Basically Rouge turns eighteen in a couple of weeks, and they don't want her under their roof anymore."

"They just kicked her out? Didn't give her a place to live or even let her finish high school? And we call Grollics monsters!" Sarah clapped her hands. "You stay here for as long as you need."

"I was thinking she could stay in the pool house," Grace said. "You know, give her a bit of privacy."

"Hmm..." Sarah nodded. "Let's see what happens at the meeting with the elders. If there are no issues, then I don't see why not."

I needed to say something. "I really appreciate this, but—"

"But nothing," Sarah said. "You need a place, we have the space."

I stopped my meagre attempt to argue. She was right and I really wanted to stay.

"The boys've left." Sarah checked her watch. "Maybe the two of you should get working as well. Caleb's pulled some books and set them on the desk for you. He thought some of them might be helpful."

I reached for Grace. "Can you not say anything to Michael yet?" I tapped the side of my head. "No sense in getting him worried."

"Good idea, but you know he's going to be ticked at me." She grinned. "No worries, I can take it. Come on."

I followed Grace into the living room and stretched to look over her shoulder at Caleb's closed office door. My heart beat switched to an erratic pattern and I wiped my palms across the front of my jeans.

Without a hint of nervousness, Grace pushed open the door and strolled inside. She chattered away about something, but I had absolutely no clue what. My senses were too busy absorbing everything in front of me.

Caleb's room was an understatement of the word office. An enticing aroma hit me before I could concentrate on the view. A hint of some kind of tobacco, old books, burning cedar, and musky vanilla infiltrated my nose. I couldn't place the exact scent but boy, was it yummy...and relaxing...and sexy...and mysterious...and... How did Caleb get any work done with these smells in the air?

The oval room had gorgeous built-in bookcases you only saw in the movies. Between the cases, a large fireplace with wood burning and popping away. I couldn't believe the amount of books. There were also bookcases which rolled around on brass bars in front of the built-in cases.

Directly across from the fireplace was a desk. *Gorgeous. Probably older than Moses.* It was made of oak with wonderful big grains and knots. On top of the desk lay a stack of books, probably fifteen but the pile looked small compared to all the books in the room. Two red leather ottoman chairs sat in front of the desk, a large antique chair behind it.

Grace plopped on one of the red leather chairs, her legs dangling over its arms. "Awesome, isn't it?"

"Really nice. I can't get over the smell."

"Kind of everything and anything rolled into one?"

"Exactly! Is it some kind of Glade Plug-in or candle?"

Grace laughed. "No plug-in or special voodoo-thing. It's Caleb."

I had never been close enough to the guy to notice. "He smells like this? No wonder Sarah tossed her Siorghra at him." If he actually smelled like this, maybe he wasn't so bad.

"I know what you're thinking," Grace said with a bemused smile. "He's hard, like he appears, but he does have a few soft spots."

"It's interesting in this room..." I glanced at my watch. "It feels like dusk, and it's only three o'clock."

"Caleb set the windows high for that effect. You can be here in the middle of the night or the middle of the day and it feels the same."

"Sorta like a casino – they say it's always bright inside so you never know the exact time!" I walked over to the desk and picked up a book. "What do you need me to do?"

"You sit in the black leather chair and start looking at books. Just browse through the ones on the desk and make a note if anything looks unique or seems similar to the Grollic book. I have no idea how you read that journal so do what you do. Whatever catches your eye or triggers something."

I nodded but had no idea whatever it was that I did. I was useless to them but wasn't about to admit that here in Caleb's sacred study. It felt wrong sitting down in Caleb's chair, but I swallowed my anxiety, determined to find something Michael could use. There were two piles of books set on the desk, a shorter one hidden behind the tall one.

The book in my hand dated back to the 1920s and had very small writing; a headache-maker. I put it aside. The next book had long paragraphs and no illustrations, boring. The third book's cover caught my eye. It had a beautiful hand drawn girl in a flowing white dress by a forest's edge. About to turn to the first page, a pair of dark black and yellow eyes peering through the forest caught my eye.

The Red Riding Hood story, but their version. Old, like the journal, but this book was written in clear calligraphy, and definitely in English. I flipped to the first page and started to read:

A beautiful young angelic girl had been sent to learn the wrongs of mankind and learn angels were different. Too tempted by lust and sins, she found a handsome man and fell in love. Afraid, she hid him in a cottage deep inside a forest.

She dressed in white, her wings packed tight almost appearing as a cape behind her. She'd been warned by the local folk to avoid the woods after dark, but held no fear. She came upon a man who was sitting upon a fallen tree. His shoulder appeared wounded so she stopped to help him. After cleaning his wound, she offered him water and food. Assured he was alright, she headed back on her way.

Unknown to the girl, the man was not as he appeared. To most he presented himself as a man and his true being was a Grollic. As the forest darkened, the man became a beast and hungered after the girl's delicious scent. It led him to a clearing in the forest where a small cottage stood. He crept inside as the scent was now familiar to him and begged to be sated.

He leapt onto the bed and attacked–only to realize after he'd killed a man with the woman's scent all over him. The mistake angered him. He hid and waited for the maiden to return.

The maiden arrived at the cottage shortly thereafter. She walked into the room and approached the bed. Seeing the bloody lifeless body on the floor, she screamed and rushed to his side. Blood seeped into her dress and wings. As she cried, the killer leapt from behind the bed.

The girl stood, unafraid and faced him defiantly. She realized the beast was the man who'd she'd helped in the forest earlier.

The Grollic hesitated as he watched the maiden's eyes turn from brown to blue. What he thought had been a cape, was actually her wings. She raced into the forest to hide. The Grollic, thinking she'd run in fear, licked his jowls in anticipation.

However, the girl surprised the beast and attacked first. Shocked, the Grollic turned back into human-form and they fought. He raped her when he gained the upper hand.

Blood gushed from a wound, she tried to cover herself and stop the bleeding. Devastated, she stared at the blood now on her hands. Her blood. Her lover killed. Everything gone. Revenge flowed through her veins. She slapped the Grollic-man, covering his mouth with her hand. Her blood on his tongue, the man swallowed and choked. He died as if poisoned.

With renewed strength and anger that seemed deep in her core, she followed the Grollic's scent and found his pack. The girl killed them all, one by one, pouring her blood into their mouths, or open wounds. She experimented with each death, learning more as each

Grollic struggled against the poison.

Her life would never be as it was. She could not return to where she had come and everything here was shattered. Before long she realized a tiny being grew in side her belly. She vowed vengeance on every Grollic for atonement – even if it took an eternity to fulfill.

Finished I sat back in the chair. How the original story got turned into a fairytale was beyond me. Grabbing the pad of paper and a pen on the desk, I jotted down to reread the Grollic version and compare. Similar story, but two totally different views.

I glanced at Grace. She sat in the red chair reading with her head down, her hair concealing her face.

I cleared my throat and she looked up. "That's a pretty gruesome story. Is this Red Riding Hood horror-story your version?"

"Our version? Does that journal tell it that differently?"

I shrugged. For some reason, I didn't think she'd believe any or agree with the other version. With both version in my head, I probably had a better idea of what really happened than anyone and yet, I wasn't so sure. "It's sort of the same but just the way they saw it."

"I never paid much attention to it. Michael and Caleb take it more seriously." Grace shrugged. "The Grollics started it all." She started reading again and didn't look up.

End of that topic, I guess. Setting the history book aside, I picked up the next one and flipped through. It looked like some genealogy or family tree. I couldn't make out many of the names except I noticed a name similar to Caleb's with a blank line beside it. I started a "maybe" pile beside the Riding Hood book. The rest of the stack didn't appear to have anything helpful I could use. The first book on the next pile had a fold on the corner of a page. Caleb's and Michael's names were handwritten on it, marked with some kind of seal.

"That's our Coven, it's like a family mark." Grace stood beside me, making me jump.

I hadn't noticed her get up. "Why are their names here and not yours?"

"Michael's expected to continue Caleb's work with the Elders. I'm expected to be mated with someone from the Higher Coven." She straightened, then shrugged with one shoulder.

"I thought –"

Grace continued, ignoring me. "The Higher Coven is the oldest group of descendents from the girl in the story you just read. They are the original and most powerful. Caleb's one of them; actually he *is* the oldest. He was one of the offspring of the Red Maiden, her firstborn. She bore sons to create soldiers in her war against the Grollics."

Wide-eyed I stared, her words completely foreign.

"There were eight of them who survived the war that killed her. She bore ten sons, two died in the first war. Three of the remaining eight have been destroyed. Now only five remain and they are the Higher Coven." She touched my shoulder. "I know this sounds confusing but there's something you need to understand. Each of the five have an understudy that's expected to take their place should anything happen."

She paused, waiting for me to pick up on something. I had no clue what. It seemed to be on the edges of my mind but I couldn't grasp what.

"*Michael* is Caleb's understudy," she said slowly.

No wonder Caleb appeared to be royalty and didn't want me, some nobody, around Michael.

Grace continued talking, "I'm expected to be mated with one of the other four understudies. This'll strengthen our power should anyone try to step out on their own or go against the Higher Coven."

"Wait a minute, back up. How can you be expected to be mated with one of them? I'm confused. What about the whole Siorghra-thing?"

"Caleb's quite sure one of the four understudies will be my match. I've never met any of them, yet. Caleb wants to keep them away for now."

"Huh? What happens if you meet someone you want to give your Siorghra to?" *Maybe the same is planned for Michael.* A stab of jealousy burned inside me. I reached for his Siorghra.

She laughed. "I've been around this long and haven't met my mate. It seems I'm still waiting to find him."

"Does he have to be one of you? Can you pass your Siorghra to a...a living human?"

She appeared unphased. "Usually no, but it does happen. For me, I don't think Caleb would allow it. He'd eliminate the problem."

I gulped. It sounded like I was pretty much screwed.

"I don't mean – shoot, I meant for me, not you. Things are different with Michael and you. Caleb sees this, and he knows how Michael feels. It's Michael's choice. If Caleb tried to force him with a decision, Michael would step down as his understudy." Grace's eyes shone with pride. "Michael's very special. He's stronger than Caleb in ways. Caleb would never go against him and try to eliminate you. The risk would be too great."

And being the kid who can read Grollic can't hurt. "So you've never fallen in love?"

"No, but believe me, I've tried." Grace giggled.

'Me, either...I've never been in love before that is."

"Before... Michael?" She smiled. A big, happy, irritating one. "One of these days you're going to have to tell me what it's like. You an' Michael. It's –"

"What time do you expect Caleb and Michael back?" I interrupted, my face burning. How could I explain something I wasn't sure of myself?

"Should be around ten or eleven, barring no complications, of course."

"Complications?"

"Yeah, you put five males—who each think they're the most powerful—in one room and things sometimes get messy. Understudies usually keep things calm, but something always comes up and ruins the mood for everyone. I think tonight was more of an emergency meeting, and Caleb has the journal. Won't be much fighting when they see it and hear Caleb's got someone who can read it."

Lucky me... always at the right place at the wrong time. "How often do they meet?"

"Like four time a year."

Sounded like a school board. "Does everyone live here, in North America?"

"No, but it isn't a problem."

I nodded, but I didn't understand. How could I even begin to fathom it? My fingers tapped against the wood of the desk. The rest of the books on the desk and none of the ones I looked through on the shelves seemed to offer anything. I had no clue what I was looking for.

The secret seemed to lie within the Grollic book of mine.

Chapter 3

The door to the office swung hard against the wall, making me jump in my seat. Caleb burst in and then stood by the doorframe with his arms crossed tight against his chest. Waiting for something. He glared in my direction.

Oh crap! I'm in his seat. Cheeks burning for the fifteenth time that day, I leapt off and hurried to the other side of the desk. Caleb said nothing, just stomped over and sat down. Michael rushed in, faster than humanly possible. His arms slipped under me, and had me in his lap as he dropped into the red seat before I even exhaled a breath. He gave me a quick squeeze before setting his hands lightly on my hips.

Sarah came in and stood behind Grace. "How'd the meeting go?"

Caleb began stacking and organizing the books around him. My little pile all scuffled in the mix. "The Higher Coven is interested in meeting Rouge. Seems no one is able to transcribe the book, and they are wondering what she may be. A few left wingers think she may be the key to winning the war." The last line carried a note of disgust.

Underneath me, Michael stiffened.

Caleb glanced up, as if sensing Michael's reaction. "Seth, of course, is quite excited to meet Rouge. He thinks she could be a traitor. Or have Grollic blood." He held his hand up to stop Grace and Sarah from speaking. "You needn't worry. Michael was very adamant she's not. He believes Rouge's pure." He loosened his tie.

"Seth suggested we test her with our blood. If she dies and stays dead, she's Grollic. If she dies and lives, she's one of us. If nothing, she's human."

"Never!" Michael's voice stayed controlled as he replied to Caleb, but under me, his entire body was tense.

I didn't know what to think. A tiny part of me hoped they'd test, and I'd turn out to be like them. Why else would I have this gift? The other ninety-five percent screamed it didn't want to freakin' die.

Caleb continued, "I disagreed. If Rouge lives, she may lose the ability to translate the book. Michael also told the elders about Damon and the misunderstanding on Halloween."

Misunderstanding? *Wait a minute, back up. Caleb thinks I'm one of them?* My heart raced with sudden excitement. Were they able to figure out if someone was one of them before they died? Now I had a million questions I wanted to ask. *Can it, Rouge. Now is not the time.*

Sarah pulled on her sleeve. "None of the elders know of the journal? Is it safe to assume the Grollics aren't aware we have it?"

"Yes," Caleb said. "Thus we need to get all the information from it as soon as we can."

In comes the Grollic whisperer.

"We still haven't seen a single beast since September, and even then, it wasn't by us." Michael's tone matched Caleb's.

"How do you know? Maybe it became distracted by *her*." Caleb pointed at me then stood. "Do you not think it's too silent? Those damn beasts don't sit quiet." He punched a fist into his palm. "They attack, and they move on. Those fools do not know how to blend into the human world without leaving a messy trail."

"It *is* very quiet." Michael sighed and pulled me closer. "Something is up. They'll make a mistake. They always do."

I stretched against Michael, my left shoulder blade burned and my neck was sore for my head turning back and forth with the conversation.

Caleb checked his phone. "Seth and Tatiana will be here in a couple of days. They'll do their scouting. Until then, it is business as usual. We cannot give away anything. We must let them think we assume nothing."

"Who's Seth?" I asked.

Grace leaned forward, resting her elbows on her knees. "Seth's one of the Elders. Tatiana wears his Siorghra." She straightened. "Speaking of guests, Rouge got kicked out of her house this afternoon."

"What?!" Michael looked at me and then glared at his twin. "Why didn't you tell me?"

"Everything's taken care of." Grace rolled her eyes. "I am capable of handling a situation. I'm not useless." Lips pursed and face tight, she pushed her shoulders back.

I wondered if she'd actually physically fight with her brother. Probably not a good idea to find out. I think Caleb and Michael underestimated Grace. I slipped off Michael's lap and stood beside the chair. "I'm eighteen next week –"

"So they kicked her out," Grace finished.

"Technically Jim kicked me out. Sally left," I joked, trying to make the situation not sound so bad.

Grace smiled. "It's better Rouge's here. If the Grollics find out about the book or her ability...she's safe with us."

I stared at the journal Caleb had set on top of the pile. "I don't want another war to start because of me or this book."

Caleb snorted. "This war has nothing to do with *you*."

"Stop!" Michael roared.

Everyone turned, surprised. More had obviously gone on at the meeting they weren't saying. I'd never seen him on edge before.

"I'm sorry—"

"Don't you dare apologize!" Michael's voice softened, "You've done nothing wrong. This war started long before you were alive and will continue long after you're gone." His eyes narrowed when he turned to Caleb. "Watch it."

"Don't you dare threaten me!" Caleb's voice turned to ice.

"Enough!" Sarah, who'd been virtually quiet until this point, spoke sharply. One word and both men set their lips into tight lines but neither said another word. Arguing sounded like a regular thing in this house. She pointed at both boys. "Let Rouge go over what she knows with Michael. They need a chance to talk. We can discuss whatever we need to in the morning. Rouge's going to stay in the pool house, so Seth and Tatianna are going to need the cabin by the lake. We need to do groceries and get things organized. Tomorrow's going to be a busy day." She walked over to the office door and motioned to Caleb and Grace. "They need a bit of space."

Michael and Caleb or Michael and me? I made a conscious effort to close my mouth after Caleb and Grace followed Sarah's order.

The sudden silence in the room made me conscious of how I probably needed a powder room break. If I looked as tired as I suddenly felt, a break wouldn't be enough, I'd need a vacation. I leaned over the desk and ran my finger over the leather of the journal. *Warm and comforting.* I almost wanted to hug it. "After watching Caleb and Grace follow Sarah like puppies, I have no intention of not doing what she says." I grinned. "Shall we get started then?"

"Touché." He picked up a red chair, and set it down beside Caleb's. He waited for me to sit and then settled in the red leather with a pen and blank notepad in hand. Reaching across, his arm brushed against mine and sending goose bumps on my skin, he set the Grollic book in front of me.

I watched his face and smiled when a single eyebrow rose.

"What?" he asked.

"Did Caleb choose you to be his understudy or did you ask?"

Michael leaned back. "Grace been filling you in on our history and boring politics?"

"Yes and no. Not boring." I lightly poked his hard chest. "Now answer the question."

He grinned, and then turned serious. "He didn't ask me nor did I offer. It was just kind of assumed. Caleb was the last to take an understudy – the others chose who they wanted and he said he just waited till the right one showed up." He shrugged.

Now came the tricky part. I had to ask about something I wasn't sure I really wanted the answer to. "Grace said she's expected to be matched with one of the understudies. I thought you were allowed to choose who you gave your Siorghra to?" I touched the necklace on my neck, knowing I'd eventually have to give it back. I pushed the heavy feelings away.

"We are. Caleb's just certain one of the understudies will be a match."

"Are the other understudies nice like you? Is there one you think'll be good for her? They're not old like Caleb, right?"

Michael sniggered. "We're talking immortality and you're worried Grace might be too young?"

"I don't want her stuck with some miserable, old, bitter guy." I swallowed, my eyes darting around the office reminding me whose room, and house, I sat in. "Not saying Caleb's like that."

Michael didn't reply—too busy laughing.

I picked up a piece of paper, crumpled it, and threw it at him.

He ducked before I'd even released it, tried to look serious for a moment, and then laughed again. He straightened. "I'd *never* let anything or anyone hurt Grace, and trust me, she'll be with who she wants to be with. She's a big girl and can make her own decisions. Nothing Caleb or I think will deter her from what she wants, no matter how powerful the opponent."

"Good."

"Good." He smiled.

"What about you?" I stared at my fingers. "Are there any sisters or family from the other understudies Caleb wants you set up with?"

"Are you *jealous*?" He had a huge smile on his face, like he'd just hit the ball out of the park.

"No! Well... maybe a little." I closed my eyes, wishing the burning on my cheeks would cool. I blinked, looking right into his beautiful ocean blue depths. "I just want to know what kind of competition I'm up against." There, I said it. I admitted I'd be willing to fight for the guy completely out of my league.

His huge smile got even bigger. "You're one of kind! You've no need to worry about anyone. They can get in line for someone else."

"You know you're crazy." I had absolutely nothing to offer. Just a silly girl with no past and not much of a future.

Michael put his hand on my chin. He leaned forward and kissed me lightly on the nose. "I'm crazy for saying we should probably get some work done. I'd rather not...but you know Caleb."

I scrunched my nose. "Okay, let's get the homework done."

He picked up the pen. "You talk, I'll write."

"Should I run and grab my laptop? I can type pretty fast."

"We'll be fine. Caleb'll prefer a handwritten copy, and we can add drawings or notes as needed."

I held the book open for a few moments, trying to decide what to do. "Let's compare their Riding Hood story to yours."

"Red Riding Hood?" A sexy eyebrow rose again.

I shrugged. "The Grollics aren't wolves but the story seems pretty similar. You've never made the comparison?"

He shook his head. "I've never heard anyone make the comparison."

"Maybe you will after I read you the book's analogue of what happened." I read him the story in the journal, amazed Michael could write so fast.

"Caleb's going to want to hear their side." He tapped the end of the pen against the notepad.

"History's complicated, don't you think? One incident can be seen completely different by ten people watching it unfold." I wondered how Caleb pictured the start of this feud. "Does each of the Higher Covens have, like, a special task or job?"

"Caleb is acting head. His temper is short but he's a brilliant leader, always three-four steps ahead of everyone. Seth, the one coming this week, is similar. He's lethal, cunning, and is very passionate." Michael chuckled. "He's an excellent scout and has a unique talent for hunting Grollics...and ladies."

In that order? "He hunts women?"

"He'd never step outside the boundaries of our laws." He grinned.

"You have laws?" I couldn't believe in today's society no one had any idea of Grollics or the ones who tried to find them. *Surreal, freakin' surreal.* "He's allowed to hunt women?"

"I'm teasing. Women tend to like him and he has no problem with the attention. He's got a special talent with the female population." Michael waved his hand. "But we do have laws. We're no different than human society. Politics is politics. Without laws, there would be chaos and disorder. Caleb is very serious about following the rules. He has no tolerance for those who do not."

If Caleb was scary, what would more of the Coven be like? "Will it bother Seth I'm here?"

"Nah...He knows his place is behind Caleb and wouldn't jeopardize anything to make Caleb angry."

"Caleb's pretty powerful, isn't he?"

"Most would never cross him unless forced to, and, honestly, he's seldom wrong."

"Does he always make everyone...so uncomfortable?" I tried hiding a yawn behind my hand.

Michael grinned, running his thumb gently along my jaw. "He doesn't try. You'll see him differently one day. Fear and respect can sometimes be interchangeable." He brushed a stray strand of hair behind my ear. "I think it's time we called it a night. Shall I tuck you in, read a fairytale, and put you to sleep?"

I yawned, unable to hide it this time. "No fairytales! My favorite's just been turned into a horror film. I'm scared what might happen to Cinderella if you tell me the truth on that one."

Chapter 4

Lying alone on Grace's bed, I tried to relax. She'd insisted on giving me some privacy, and the amount of winking and nudging she'd given me before leaving the room had me in jitters. I pulled the covers tightly around me and forced my eyes shut, every muscle tight. So what if Michael came in? *It's not like you have to sleep with him.* I never gone down that road and knew I wasn't ready.

At the sound of a knock, I jumped. Michael poked his head in and smiled when he saw me. He walked in and closed the door behind him. He wore only a pair of cotton pajama bottoms, and those seemed to show off his sleek build even more. Shirtless, the tanned muscles from his abs, his chest, and his shoulders, belonged on the cover of a magazine.

He stood by the bed, an amused look on his face most likely due to me blatantly checking him out. I scooted to the far side of the bed, thankful the sheets were cool, as I'd suddenly grown warm. He hopped on top of the sheets and lay down, resting his hands behind his head as he crossed his ankles. I couldn't stop staring; he looked like a Greek god. Change that, he made Greek gods look like poor, lowly little boys.

He sniffed the air. "You smell different."

"I brushed my teeth."

"No, it's not that. I didn't notice it earlier because of Caleb's office but I can smell it now."

My face burned a few degrees higher. *Grace, I'm so going to beat the crap out of you.* "It's perfume," I mumbled. Would he still like me if I murdered his sister? Mind you, it really wouldn't be murder if she's legally dead already.

He inhaled. "Pretty. What kind?"

How he kept a straight face was beyond me. "Grace put you up to this?" I leaned on top of his chest, tapping my finger where his heart rested. "The truth."

He chuckled. "She may've mentioned to ask the name of your perfume."

"She's dead tomorrow. Double dead." I rolled off him.

"Hey, get back here!" Michael pulled me back on top of him.

It knocked me breathless, and not from his strength. I could feel his rock hard chest underneath my thin pajama top. New, incredible sensations coursed through my body, through my veins, in my stomach and lower. The little electric shocks when we touched hands were nothing compared to this. I searched his face for a sign that showed if my body had given away any of its secrets.

He smiled and kissed me lightly on the lips, keeping his eyes open. "I knew there was something special about you that night in the cemetery." He shook his head. "What kind of girl goes running around dead people?"

"Not many."

"And you're still doing it."

"Sure. 'Cept now, it's a hundred times more interesting. Before, I just liked the peace and quiet." I interlaced my fingers on top of his chest and rested my chin on them.

"Silly girl." He twirled a strand of my hair around his finger.

"You know," I swallowed and whispered, "I-I'd give you my Siorghra if I had one."

He pulled me tight and kissed the top of my head. After a few moments, he spoke quietly, "Can I ask you a question?"

"Ask away, I'll tell you anything you want to know." My heart stepped up its pace a few notches.

"What's the name of the perfume you're wearing?"

I pretended to shoot him a dirty look and slid away from him to settle on my side of the bed. "I'm going to skin Grace alive tomorrow." I rolled back and punched him in the arm, grinning despite his uncanny ability to ruin a perfectly good moment.

"You said you'd tell me." He snuggled against me and pushed his face under my shoulder. His hot breath fanned my back as he chuckled. He popped his head up. "Please?"

I rubbed my face. "Fine, but you can't mention it again. Or laugh." I ran a finger across his soft lips. "No laughing."

"Scouts' honor."

"You have no honor." I sighed. "Fine. It's...Eternity."

He burst out laughing, shaking the entire bed. "Sorry. I-I'm much b-better now. Is this something you bought before, or after you met me?" He tried to sound serious, but the bed still trembled beneath us.

"Way before. It's going in the garbage tomorrow." I debated about turning to the wall and pretending to go to sleep. *It is kinda funny.* Not that I'd admit it out loud.

"No, keep it. Please. The smell suits you. I do like it."

I didn't reply. It seemed like a great idea to dump the bottle over Grace's head. "It's my turn to ask you a question."

"Fair is fair. Ask away." He tucked his hands behind his head.

I chewed the inside of my cheek, trying to pick the right question. *Fun's done, I want to know stuff.* "What happened...the night you and Grace... you know?"

Michael lay quiet. Then he slowly sat up and leaned over to turn the light off.

Wrong question. Instantly I regretted opening my mouth. *Me and my great mood killers.*

He took one of my hands in his and spoke in a quiet voice. "It was eighteen seventy. I remember the exact date because Congress amended the constitution so African-Americans would be allowed to vote. During dinner, my father was ecstatic as he had always believed in equal rights. He told my mother he believed women would have their right to vote shortly as well. They were so amazing, my parents. You've never seen loyalty and love like theirs. No Siorghra could ever come close.

"It was early summer, the strawberries had just come into season and their smell hung in the air around the house. It was my mother's favorite time of year and after cleaning the dishes, she went to sit on the front porch to watch the fireflies dance. My father sat in the living room reading and journaling. Grace and I were in the back of the house in the kitchen, playing cards, and if you ask her, she'll tell you she was beating me."

He chuckled, but it sounded forced. I lay without moving, afraid to hear what happened next, but yearning to know more.

"I didn't hear them come to the house. You know animals when they hunt, quiet and cunning as they stalk. Only, I have no idea if they were hunting us, or if our plantation sat in the wrong spot at the wrong time. If only they'd just passed us by. They must've smelled mother. She barely screamed before it got cut off." Michael shuddered. "It was an awful sound. My father jumped up and ran to the front door. I was halfway out of my seat when the door flew open and three enormous monsters jumped in. Awful, devil-sent beasts. They killed him like he was nothing.

"Four more came in through the front with, you aren't going to believe this, a man. I was too shocked to even move. Grace whimpered and the beasts heads p-popped up at the s-sound."

The break in his voice tore at my heart. I transported back in time, watching the horror like a fly on the wall.

Michael continued, his eyes shining. "I scrambled in front of her, not sure if I would be able to protect her, but was not going to fall without a fight. There was a knife on the counter I picked up. The man spoke in some weird language, and... and the Grollics all dropped to their haunches, as if waiting.

"I've somehow blanked out what happened next. For years I've tried to recall but it's a blur. I remember his movements were fast like ours are now, but he led the Grollics like he was one of them. I was human, no match against him. He wrestled the knife away before I could even use it. He turned and stabbed me."

Michael swallowed, loud against the quiet of the room. "It was a fatal wound to my chest, one blow and I was lying on the floor, bleeding. I could feel my life fading. I begged him to leave Grace. He laughed viciously and taunted me – telling me I would get to watch him rape and kill my sister before I died. Then he grabbed and flung her to the floor like a rag doll, holding the knife so it stabbed her in her back as she fell, paralyzed." Michael sighed, a long shaky one. "Grace never said a word, or had a single tear in her eye. She smiled at me before spitting in the man's face and closed her eyes. I shut mine as well and gave in as death would be better than watching her die."

Tears ran silently down my face. *What a horrible, horrible memory.*

Michael shifted slightly. "I don't know what exactly happened next. All I know is I heard Sarah's sweet voice. My first coherent thought: I'm in heaven and that's the voice of an angel. That thought quickly changed when she said the woman out front, my mother, had been attacked by the Grollics, and killed my father. She grabbed my hand, and promised to protect us. She'd explain what we could not understand."

He lay quiet, a shaky finger trailing down my arm.

I pulled free, put my arms around his shoulders and hugged him. "What a terrible story," I whispered.

"I haven't talked about it in forever. It no longer seems real. It...It feels like someone else's life now. Thank goodness we had Sarah there to explain the, you know, *after*." He shrugged. "It was about fifteen years later when Caleb found us."

"Did you ever find the man who killed..." I couldn't complete the sentence. "Or the Grollics who attacked the house?"

"I tried for years. Grace begged me to let it go and move forward. Eventually I stopped searching." He pulled me tight against him and kissed the top of my head. "I did find out my mother had been raped the day of her wedding. It didn't lead me any closer to the beasts or the man. They had nothing to do with her rape or our birth. I never dug deeper."

"I'm sorry."

"Pardon?"

I could feel his head lift to try and see my face. "I'm sorry you and Grace had to suffer before you died."

"You're a silly-soft little girl. Don't be sorry. It's in the past and it brought me to you." His head dropped back onto the pillow. "It doesn't matter anymore."

I didn't believe him. It still did matter and, one day, Michael was going to hunt down the truth.

Chapter 5

In the morning I woke in the same position I had fallen asleep. Michael lay quiet beside me, his fingers tracing my shoulder, along my tank top strap, across my shoulder blade and making a circle somewhere around my birthmark. I didn't want to move or open my eyes. *Laying here forever suits me fine.* Maybe I could get another ten minutes of bliss, if I pretended to sleep. A small sigh escaped my lips as I snuggled closer to him.

"I'd gladly lie here with you all day, but Grace won't get out of my head. She keeps asking if you're awake."

"Hmm," I murmured. "If I tap your head, can you tell her I'm snoozing for twenty minutes?"

Michael stayed quiet a moment, obviously talking to Grace.

"It's fascinating you can talk to her in your head." I stretched my legs, but not wanting to leave the warmness his body offered.

"You kill me." He laughed. "We're reincarnate some kind of angel offspring fighter beasts referred to as Grollics, and you think it's cool I can communicate with my twin? You continue to amaze me." He lifted me up on top of him so my head was inches from his. "Most twins have their own language or way of communicating with each other. It's not so unusual. I would thi—"

I kissed him on the lips. I didn't know why I had no problem with the fighting Grollic thing, my gut feeling wanted them dead as well. Trying to remember whatever else Michael had just said seemed beyond my scope at the moment. Waking up beside him was far more interesting.

Minutes later, Michael held me slightly away from him and groaned. "Grace is bugging me again. She can hear we're awake and warned she's barging in the room in two minutes. Either we need to get up or," he said, grabbing my elbow, "we can give her something to—"

I pulled back and jumped off the bed. "I'm up! I'm going to the bathroom. You do what you want!"

As I closed the door, a soft thump hit the back side of it. *A pillow.* I smiled in the mirror and gave myself two thumbs-up.

Twenty minutes later I emerged from Grace's bedroom showered and dressed in my favorite red sweater and jeans. Down in the kitchen Michael, Grace, and Sarah sat talking quietly.

Michael went to the counter and offered me a croissant. "I made you coffee." He poured me a cup. "Milk and sugar's on the island by Grace."

I settled down and dropped in three heaping teaspoons of sugar and lots of milk.

"Wow, you like a lot of sweetness," Grace said, watching me.

"Just tastes better." I took a sip, trying not to shudder. Michael still made lousy coffee, no wonder I was the only one drinking it.

Michael sat beside me. "Sarah and Grace organized the pool house for you. It's officially your place, but as long as Damon or any other Grollic is around, I'm not letting you out of my sight."

Sarah opened her mouth, but Michael held a hand up. "For the sake of argument, she turns eighteen in six days." He smiled and bit into his croissant.

"If it's okay with Rouge," Sarah replied smugly. "She might want space. And you do exactly as she says."

They all looked at me.

They wanted me to tell them how I felt about Michael in a room with no adult supervision? *Not going to happen.* "I'm just incredibly thankful you guys are letting me stay. You're the ones with Grollics chasing you. Whatever it takes to keep you all safe, I'm cool with."

Grace laughed. "You're worried about us? So cute."

Michael harrumphed. "Want to see the pool house?"

"Sure." I pushed the three-quarter full mug away.

We headed out the sliding doors in the kitchen into the cool morning air. Without a coat, I had no problem snuggling into Michael's warm, outstretched arm. Walking around the Olympic size pool, I stumbled as I stared at my temporary home.

Simple stucco walls with large windows and a heavy slate roof. The place had to be eight hundred square feet, and Grace said it was small. The windows reflected the closed pool. They were obviously the one-sided kind—you could see out from the inside.

Michael handed me a key from his pocket. "Voila. Your castle."

Too shocked to reply, I unlocked and stepped through the door. The open beige and brown painted room had wood flooring, a king size futon set in front of a humongous TV. Behind the couch, a pair of bar stools sat neatly tucked under a marble counter. Standing on my toes, I could see a small chrome mini fridge and dishwasher. I sniffed, the place smelled like lemons and cleaning detergents.

"Grace brought your stuff." Michael pointed to a dresser neatly set against the wall. "The bathroom has a large closet where your hang up clothes are. There's also a washer and dryer in there too." He grabbed his cell phone out of his back pocket and checked the screen. "Do you think you'll be alright for a bit? Caleb needs me. I can send Grace over if you'd like."

"I don't mind hanging out here on my own for a bit. Unless you think Grace might be offended."

Michael laughed. "She's a big girl. She can watch from the window." He pushed me gently toward the futon. "Go. Relax. I'll be back as soon as I'm done." He quietly closed the door behind him.

Alone, I sat down and put my feet on top of the coffee table. My right ankle slipped against a magazine. Leaning forward, I caught it just before it hit the floor.

The Grollic journal.

Grace must've put it and my laptop on the coffee table thinking I'd want to do some work.

Maybe on my own, in the quiet of the room, I could figure something else out from the book. Getting up I went and checked the fridge and grabbed a bottle of water, then settled back down.

I flipped open to the front page. *Might as well start at the beginning.* I didn't understand any of the writing, but maybe using the Internet I might find a word or two which might explain something—anything. I flipped the laptop open and as I waited for the computer to load, I turned to look at the first few pages and diagrams of the journal. It all looked foreign to me.

I came to the drawing of the Grollic and man. A caption underneath read: *Vargulf Bentos Monstrum.* "Whatever that means," I mumbled to myself. So I did what any normal human being would do. I googled the words.

The last word brought me to links on monsters but none of it made sense. All I could find on Bentos was some relation to a Portuguese name. "These words have no connection to the drawings," I mumbled.

The following page continued in the strange language. One underlined phrase made me curious. *Vilkacis diakonos.* I typed it into the Internet. The phrase "Wolf eyes" seemed the going theme for Vilkacis. *The Grollics freaky yellow eyes looked like some kind of wolf or scary beast.* I typed in diakonos and the word I could make out, and still made no sense was: service. It was like trying to connect the dots without the numbers.

Afternoon faded into early evening before I realized how long I'd been working. Flipping the lights on, I made some pasta from the cupboard and turned the futon into a bed to get more comfortable. A knock on the door startled me, causing me to throw the bed cover instead of shake it out to flutter onto the mattress.

Michael poked his head through the door. "Hi, beautiful. You should lock the door if you're on your own."

"You've never knocked before." I smiled and hopped onto the bed. "Do you honestly think a locked door will stop one of you or some Grollic?"

"This place is actually equipped with bullet proof tamper glass and the door is –"

"Why in the world?" They were immortal, why need protection?

He chuckled and gave a half shrug. "Caleb's business creates and sells all sorts of inventions. He likes trying them out at home."

"He's got a business on top of the whole Coven-thing?"

Michael laughed. "He's a genius and likes making money. Plus, it's a good cover for the Coven. Interesting board meetings." He sat on the bed and squeezed my hand. "I won't bore you with details."

"I don't think you can ever be boring." I stifled back a yawn, turning red since I had been serious when I spoke. My tired body thought otherwise.

"Liar." He winked.

"Honest. I've just been reading and searching the internet for anything I could find."

"Any luck?"

"Nothing you don't already know." My gaze travelled along the outline of his body, the perfect blond hair, broad shoulders with their little boney parts sticking out over sculpted muscles. I reached out and brushed my hand over his back, enjoying the warmth that seeped through his shirt onto my hands and deep into my core. "What's it like, having already died once?"

"Fascinated, aren't you?" He crawled over my legs and settled down beside me. "It's hard to explain... my human life seems so long ago. I've forgotten a lot of things. My living memories seem like trying to remember something you did as a child. Sometimes a picture triggers a thought or memory. Everything is so much easier now." He ran his fingers through his hair. "It's weird. I remember my parents and the day we were killed very clearly – better than Grace. I can remember everything from that day –the sound of my mother's voice, the sweet smell from the nearby fields, how dark the night became, all of it. I'm not sure why. I've asked Caleb, but he didn't have an answer either."

"At least things are better as you are now. All you're little powers and the not dying part makes things easier."

"I wouldn't say that." He sighed, long and deep. "I've adapted and accepted what I am. At first I loved it, then resented it, then accepted it. However, there's no going back. I'll never have the luxury of growing old, or having children, or grandchildren. When I was eighteen or nineteen years old, I very much wanted to marry and have kids. To buy land and build a house with my own hands, set roots down." He lay quiet for a moment. "What about you; have you ever thought about children?"

"The past seventeen years I've resented being born. There's no way I'd want a kid to grow up the same way I have."

"It wouldn't be like that."

"Michael, I don't know who my parents are, or if they are even alive. I spent my entire life in the foster system. I wasn't a bad kid, just unlucky I guess. When I was twelve, I spent the summer with a pretty messed up family. The foster parents had a seventeen-year-old boy who was really screwed up. He didn't like me and spent most of the summer trying to make it torture for me. Stupid things at first, like pushing me down the last two steps when we came down the stairs or kicking me in the shins when his parents weren't looking. It was my fault as I never said anything and he grew bolder. He would sneak into my room at night when I was sleeping and would light matches to burn my arm or put pins in my bed – stupid things. I just kept quiet because I thought he'd eventually give up. I figured he would get bored because I wouldn't cry or tell on him.

"It was the last weekend before he had to go back to his boarding school. He snuck into my room while I was sleeping and hit me on the head with some kind of crow bar or bat. Whatever it was, it knocked me out. The next time I opened my eyes, I was in a hospital and it was four days later. I was beaten up pretty bad and had lost a lot of blood. The pity in the doctor's eyes was worse than the physical pain. I've got liquid courage; I'm useless at standing up to anyone. So, not really the child bearing type." I'd never told anyone that story. I couldn't believe I'd just said it now. Michael had just been gone for a bunch of hours and here I tell a gruesome story of the last foster home before Jim and Sally's? *Smooth move, dummy.*

Michael seemed ten degrees warmer than before. The brightness in his eyes confirmed his anger.

"It's a stupid story. I'm just not interested in being a mother." I wasn't going to tell Michael if something ever happened to me and my kid got stuck in the foster system, I'd roll over in my grave.

"What's the boy's name? I'll find him and pay him a visit."

I put my hand on Michael's leg and traced my thumb along his jeans. "It wouldn't fix what's already broken. That boy was pretty screwed up and should have gotten help years before I came along. The following summer he was with some buddies in the woods and the reports said he was attacked by a bear. He got mauled so bad he died from the injuries." I shuddered, remembering the article in the newspaper. "I survived, moved on, and let go a long time ago. That's all it is now, just a story about some silly girl who learned a very hard lesson."

Michael cupped my cheek with his hand. "No one's ever going to hurt you. You stand up and protect yourself with no shame or fear. There aren't a lot of people who are fearless. It's an incredible strength to have."

Fearless? I liked the sound of that. "I never had anything to lose in my life – until now. You."

"Well, you'll never lose me. Wait, let me rephrase that; I sound like some sort of stalker. As long as you'll have me, you are never going to get rid of me." He pounded his heart. "We immortals have longevity on our side."

I laughed. "I'll love you forever if you'd like."

Michael's pupils grew big. For a moment he said nothing. "You've got my Siorghra so I figured it's kind of assumed."

Except you didn't put it on me, Grace did. I smiled but kept my mouth shut – until I thought of something else. "Did you have a girlfriend back when...back before?"

He nodded. "I did."

"Did you um... have you... were you *intimate* with your girlfriend back then?" *Holy anciently word, dipstick!* The skin on my face and scalp tingled, running all the way down my neck and back, even my shoulder blade burned. If hands could blush, mine were probably doing it right now.

Michael didn't appear to notice, or at least he acted like he hadn't. "Things were different back then. In those days it was frowned upon."

He offered nothing more and didn't ask me about my intimate doings. Maybe he'd done it a lot since dying and knew I was virgin territory. It probably flashed across my forehead like a billboard sign. I wasn't embarrassed about being a virgin, just humiliated on how I'd brought the subject up.

I faked a yawn, which turned into one of those huge, long ones.

Michael smiled and grabbed the duvet. He tucked me in like a cocoon. "You try and sleep. It's getting late. Tomorrow Seth and Tatiana are coming and you've got school the following day. We need to be organized in case Damon's there."

"Do they want to meet me?"

"Seth wants to see the parts of the book you can read."

"And Tee-Anna?"

He paused. "Tatiana's curious."

"About me?"

"No. Why I'm taken with a mortal."

"So am I," I whispered, wondering the same thing, and curious to know how abnormal it was for them.

Chapter 6

Morning came and I didn't even remember closing my eyes. A small note on the pillow beside me, written in scriptive writing, read:

Be back shortly. Caleb called. ' M

Grabbing a pair of jeans and red knitted sweater, I dressed and then straightened the futon. On the other side of the window glass, white fluffy powder covered the ground. Michael came toward the pool house, wearing a pair of dark jeans and black leather jacket.

I opened the door. "Mornin'."

"Heyya. Sleep alright?" He kissed me softly, his lips refreshingly cool. He straightened. "Seth and Tatiana are here. They'd like to meet you."

"—and I'm just dying to see them." I laughed nervously.

"Best not let them know – or at least not in those exact words." He squeezed my shoulder and grinned.

"Let's go then. No sense in keeping them waiting."

Michael held me back. "It's really cold out, like ten degrees below zero and that's not even including the wind-chill. You need a coat and boots. Those sneakers are useless with a foot and half of snow."

"It's all I've got." I'd left my boots at Jim and Sally's, along with my winter coat.

"Great. All Grace needs is an excuse to shop." He opened the door and turned around. "Hop on my back."

"Excuse me?"

"The snow's deep, I'll piggyback you to the house."

"Nice first impression. No thanks."

"Better than cold, wet feet followed by a crappy cold and Caleb's comments."

"Piggyback it is then."

He speed walked around the pool and I hid my head against his shoulder. It was freezing out. I said a silent thank-you when we went into the kitchen and no one was there.

Michael set me down and took my hand. "You ready?"

I swallowed and tucked a loose strand of hair behind my ear. I gave a brisk nod and we walked into the living room.

A tall woman stood by Grace, not facing me. The moment I entered, her back stiffened. Spinning around, she glared at me, her eyebrows drawn together. This had to be Tatiana.

Her black dress clung so tightly to her perfect body; I wondered how she got in or out of it. Tanned, like the others, but her hair was long and so black, it seemed blue. A shine from her silver antique necklace caught my eye, which I quickly dropped my gaze after realizing it looked like I was staring at her large breasts. Her thigh-high black boots shouted ass-kicker. Tatiana was stunning but terrifying at the same moment.

I stepped closer to Michael – more behind him than beside him.

"Tatiana," Michael said. Her sapphire blue eyes broke from me and looked at him, turning a few shades of lighter to a topaz color.

"She's prettier than I imagined." She spoke as if I wasn't in the room.

"*She* has a name. It's Rouge." The static in his voice made even me shudder.

Tatiana tsked, her eyes flitting back and forth from me to Michael. "Fine. Roww-*ge*. It's nice to see you. There's been a lot of talk."

I stepped away from Michael and despite my first hesitation, held my hand out. "Hello. You're different than I expected too." I figured she could read into that whatever way she wanted. My gut reaction—I didn't like her either.

Her warm, long fingers brushed against mine, but quickly pulled away like I burned her. She opened her mouth but said nothing, only glanced towards the closed office door.

Straining to hear something I couldn't, I jumped slightly when the door opened and Caleb walked out. Tatiana immediately retreated beside Grace, her body purposely angled so her back faced me.

Behind Caleb a tall, young man followed. *Seth*.

It took sheer will power to fight the urge to step back behind Michael again. These two strangers were friends – family – to Michael and his family but they were terrifying in a way I couldn't explain.

Caleb moved to the desk and sat down. Seth leaned against the door frame, blatantly looking me up and down. Dressed in black like Tatiana, his bright blue eyes danced against the darkness of his hair and clothes. A silver chain hung around his neck, his Siorghra disappeared inside his shirt.

"Seth!" Michael spoke sharply.

All heads swung my way. The pity, dislike, curiosity, annoyance in their eyes became too much.

Nervous but annoyed at constantly being judged, I moved beside Michael. "I'm the Grollic-reader, so what?" I wouldn't mind shoving the journal down the new girl's throat and seeing if it had the same affect as Grollic's blood. *Where did that just come from?*

Seth stepped in front of Caleb. "My dear, don't be angry. We're simply intrigued. You're lovely, and so...fresh." Seth's voice could send any female's heart racing. It was deep and husky with an accent I couldn't pinpoint. He had the charisma and confidence a lot of women would follow without question.

His hands neatly in his pockets, Seth ambled toward us. Michael exhaled forcefully through his nose.

"Ach, Michael." Seth shook his head slightly. "You needn't worry. I shall be on my best behavior." He took my hand and pressed his warm, soft lips against my skin. "I can see how you have become infatuated with this little prize. I commend you on keeping her a secret—"

"Enough!" Michael said quietly, but it felt like he'd roared the words and cut Seth off.

"My apologies." He smiled at Michael and moved beside Tatiana.

"Well, where is this book the girl can read?" Tatiana snapped.

Caleb spoke. "Tatiana, you are a guest in my house." He looked at Seth. "Upset Michael and you will disappoint and anger this house, especially me."

What the heck? These people are wacked. I had no idea what was going on or why Caleb suddenly felt the need to protect. However, the needles in his voice proved to me he meant business.

Nobody moved. Heat began crawling up my neck and onto my cheeks. My heart hammered so loud I was sure everyone could hear it. "The journal's in the pool house."

"Grace," Michael said. "Please grab it." She nodded and immediately left. I stood by him, uncomfortable at the strange silence in the room. Thank goodness Grace raced back before I lost my courage.

"Here," Grace whispered and handed me the journal.

The soft binding calmed my racing heart. Encouraged, as if it held some sort of inner power for me, I moved over to the desk. "Seth. Is it ok I call you Seth, or do you prefer something else?" I turned to Tatiana for her approval, thinking she might appreciate it. She gave a curt nod. Score one for me.

"Call me anything you'd like, sweetca—" Seth stopped and grinned. "My bad."

I set the journal on the desk. "It's apparently written in some ancient text. I tried finding something about it on the internet and came up empty handed." I flipped open to the first section. "This part of the book is all foreign to me."

Seth walked over and began turning the pages. Michael came and stood on the other side of me, not saying a word.

"Show me what you can read," Seth said. "This entire book's in the same language."

I opened to the middle. "These pages, about twenty, are in English. I can't explain why I can read it, or why none of you see it."

Tatiana appeared on the other side of Seth. "It's obvious. You've Grollic blood in you."

Seth scoffed. "She's no monster." He touched my hand, covering it with his own.

"I had no idea Grollics existed till this summer." I tried to ignore the warmth Seth's hand offered, and the revulsion to jerk my hand away. The tug of war raged on inside my body.

"What about your parents?" Tatiana asked. "Grollics reproduce – you may be just a pup, unchanged. How old are you?"

"What does that have to do with anything?" However the possibility of what she suggested shook my insides. If I'm Grollic, Michael would be the enemy. I couldn't be. *I'd feel it...somehow. Right?*

Seth answered before I managed to remind myself to breathe. "Wrong again, Tat. With Grollic blood, she wouldn't want to be here." He glanced at my neck. "And, she couldn't wear a Siorgha without excruciating pain."

If looks could kill, Tatiana would've just put me six feet under.

"I don't know why I can read it." I pointed to the book. "I found it this September and only started looking at it this week. Michael's helping me sort it out. See if I can figure out how to read the rest." I moved my hand from underneath Seth's and put it in Michael's. I wanted both of them to know who my alliance was with.

"Something's not right." Tatiana pursed her lips tight together for a moment. "No mere human picks up a book like this by chance.

Nor should she be able to read it." The girl was determined to make her point.

Surprisingly, Caleb spoke. "Michael trusts her, and that is enough. I have not asked you here to question the girl, but to find the Grollics. Your job is to scout. If you can't do that, then you are not needed."

Wow, the big guy came to my defense? Maybe Caleb wasn't so bad after all. *Maybe.* He looked pretty pissed staring at me down the bridge of his long nose.

"I always enjoy you boldness, Caleb," Seth said. "It's no problem. We are simply covering all bases. One would hate to be blindsided by love." He winked at Michael.

Michael seemed ready to pounce.

"Gorgeous," Seth said to Grace, "would you care to show me around the area and fill me in on where you think monsters may be? Caleb, I believe we've concluded the personal business we needed to discuss today?"

Caleb gave a curt nod and walked to his office, closing the door. Grace and Seth headed towards the front door, chatting quietly.

Michael squeezed my hand. "I just need to talk to Seth a moment. I'll be right back."

I nodded, picked up the Grollic book, and headed to the kitchen's back door.

Tatiana followed, but I ignored her. She wanted to try and intimidate me, which annoyed me.

"Is there something you want to say?" I tried unsuccessfully to keep the anger out of my voice.

"Words cannot explain what I think of you," she hissed.

"Sorry to hear you feel that way. It wou—"

"I'm not finished!" She stepped closer, her hands on her hips. "You do not belong here, or with this Coven! I don't know what Michael is thinking, but believe me, you won't last! You're a danger to everyone around you. You are nothing."

Last freakin–straw. I'd moved across country, then got kicked out. I'd finally found the closest thing I've ever had to a family and this... this stupid girl wants to take it away. Over my dead body. "You know nothing about me, or my relationship with Michael. This is not your place to judge, so *back off!*"

"Are you challenging me?" Her eyes turned a darker blue, making the faint line between pupil and iris impossible to see.

"How dense do you think I am?" I scoffed. "You think I don't know I stand no chance against you? You don't like me, fine. However, you're going to piss off a lot of people in this house if you do anything to me. I wouldn't want to be in your shoes at this moment." I grabbed the back door handle, cold air blasting across my face. "You may have the power but I control it."

We stood silent, staring at each other, the antique clock hanging on the wall chimed the quarter to warning. Tatiana's eyes faded to a lighter shade of blue. I had no idea what she thought I meant by the last line I'd just said. I wanted to say she had strength and ability on her side but I had the power to tell Michel or Caleb and get her booted out. I was pretty sure that would happen if I had a legit complaint.

I sighed. Maybe we could find some common ground. "I'm not asking you to like me, but if there is something I can do – even if it's insignificant – I'm going to help Michael."

She spun around and stalked to the back door, slamming it just as Michael walked into the kitchen.

"Where's the fire?" Michael watched her go, then looked at me. "Everything alright?"

"Just peachy."

He came over and hugged me. "Tat's just jealous–everyone likes you, even Caleb and Seth."

"I think Seth likes any, and every, chick."

"True. He does have a way with the ladies."

"Tatiana's one angry female. Who put the burr under her saddle?"

Michael laughed. "She did that all on her own. She can be difficult, but she's good for Seth. She keeps him in line. Her problem now is that she sees you as an obstacle. She doesn't like humans – particularly pretty girls who apparently have the head Coven wrapped around her finger."

Chapter 7

More snow fell during the night, which made the drive to school in Grace's Smartcar an adventure. We got stuck five minutes from school.

Grace, or any other of the Knightlys, failed to mention their unbelievable strength. I guess I kind of assumed they were strong, but to sit in the car and watch skinny Grace lean back into the snow bank and push the bumper with her legs till pulled free, only made me snort in disbelief.

Thank goodness no one was around to see. We arrived twenty minutes late, not only because of the car ride but also Michael's verbal concern about letting Grace go to school without protection. He kept mumbling about a gut feeling that had something to do with both him and his sister.

Half the buses hadn't arrived yet so our lateness didn't cause any eyebrow raising. Simon stood leaning on my locker.

"Hey girlie- girls!" He grinned. "Crazzzeee snow, 'eh?"

"The snow's playing havoc with my little car!" Grace pretended to whine, nudging me.

I tried hiding a smile, but the corners of my mouth kept twitching. "The snow's awesome. It brings out the superhero in all of us." I glance at Grace from the corner of my eye. It felt good to tease her and relax. Grace burst out laughing.

Simon rolled his eyes, obviously not getting our joke. "I think you two have been snorting the white stuff outside."

"The s-snow?" Another fit, Grace and I were beside ourselves.

Grace straightened and took a long breath. "Back when I was a kid, we used to have the best snow storms. Michael and I used to have snowball fights that were crazy." She stopped smiling and a look of sadness crossed her face.

Simon's poked her shoulder oblivious to change of her mood. "We should have a snowball fight at lunch in the courtyard!"

Grace perked up. "I'd kick your butt!"

"You... and whose army?"

She did a mock bow. "Challenge accepted. You. Me. Lunch. Outside."

"I'll go easy on you."

Grace pulled my arm to drag me towards our first class. "You're toast," she teased over her shoulder.

"Remember, there can only be one!" Simon hollered, his pointer finger sticking above the crowd of students going the opposite direction.

"I hope you go easy on him," I whispered as we walked into the classroom. "If someone no—"

"Sweetie," Grace teased. "I know how to play the game."

The morning flew, with no Damon making an appearance. Grace stood waiting by our lockers at the lunch buzzer. She already had her coat on, twirling her scarf around her arm and unwrapping it, only to twirl it again.

"Hurry. I need to find the best spot in the courtyard before Simon!"

"I'm not going outside, I don't have boots."

"Don't worry, I'll clear a little area for you to stand. We'll need a referee."

"Dream on! That'll just make me the perfect target."

Simon popped his head around the corner, a tuke pulled tight over his ears. "Are you stallin'?"

"No way."

"We'd better set some ground rules before we head out."

"You scared you might get hurt?" Grace grinned and slammed her locker.

"Only thinking of you, sunshine."

"After our water balloon fight last summer, I think it's you who should be worrying."

"Guys!" I interrupted, laughing. "I'll watch from inside the cafeteria. I've no intention of being anywhere near either of you."

They raced out the door as I walked to the cafeteria. I bought lunch and set my tray down by one of the windows facing the courtyard. Simon and Grace had already taken spots behind two overturned picnic tables and were hurling snowballs at lightning speed toward each other. You could hear their laughter through the windows.

"Sitting alone? Found out your friends aren't really trustworthy?"

I froze at the sound of Damon's voice. *Play it cool. He has no idea I know.*

"Who're the brainless idiots outside?"

My heart thundering loud enough to shake the walls, I kept my eyes on those figures outside. He sat down a few spaces beside me. Out of the corner of my eye, I shot a glance his way and almost choked on my soup from the amount of food on his tray – enough to feed a small nation.

"H-Hungry?" I had to say something since I now couldn't stop staring.

"– and you're still alive to eat," he retorted.

"If you call what the cafeteria serves food, then I guess I can." Pretending to joke, instead of following the urge to get up and walk way, was harder than I thought.

He set his fork down and turned to face me. "I heard you broke up with your boyfriend."

What? I almost opened my mouth to argue and realized he had no idea of what had happened over the Christmas holidays. "It's none of your business."

"Whatever. You're better off." He turned back to his food and stared out the window. "Oye! Simon just got nailed in the face! Who's he fighting? Ryan?" He'd scarfed down a plate of some kind of noodle in tomato sauce, the red reminding of a snarl against his lips.

"No...Grace."

"She's still here? Crap! Simon's going to get smoked." He grimaced and pushed his tray away like the food.

Play it cool. Act like you don't know anything. "He's being way too easy on her."

"So now you're the expert." Damon turned to glare at me, apparently no longer interested in the snowball match. He picked a sandwich off his plate and started chewing again.

Like a twig being snapped, I couldn't take it anymore. *Grollic or not, the guy's an ass.* "What's your problem? I get it that you don't like Grace – she turned you down a while back – but don't you think you should just get over it? Leave her, and me, alone." I held my breath. *Where the heck that'd come from?*

His eyes narrowed to slits and some massive vein started throbbing in his neck. "You really that stupid? Do you not see what is right in front of your eyes?"

"I know exactly what's in front of me right now." Why couldn't I just keep my mouth shut? You'd think with all the feet I'd stuffed inside of it, I'd know better.

Damon just shook his head and took a long drink. "What in the world would you want with them?"

What had I done? What would—

"—If you're that stupid, maybe you should stay with them." He interrupted my train of thought and started on another plate of food.

"Who are you to judge?" Screw him. I had some serious power-people to back me up. *My boyfriend can kick your sorry, hairy*

Grollic ass.

"You're completely clueless. It's people like you who make the human race look bad."

"The human race? I guess that doesn't include you." *Oh crap. Too far, Rouge, too far.*

His head whipped around so fast I thought he'd break his own neck.

A shiver ran down my spine when I thought what Caleb might think of my mouth. I tried backing up and coving my tracks. "I-I'd hardly call you human – you're the rudest, most annoying person I've ever met!"

He tilted back and started laughing, which came out more like barking. At the sound, Grace threw a wild snowball way over Simon. Her hands shot up in the air in surrender. She ran to the backdoors and inside without a second glance at the surprised Simon.

"Looks like your gal-pal doesn't want you hanging out with me," Damon sneered.

"Who'd want to hang with you? You're like the town bully who never grows up—never has any friends. Ends up with nothing. Not a damn thing."

"Better than being dead."

I turned to face him, trying to look as pissed-off as I could. My shoulders burned, all the way down to my spine. "Are you threatening me? Or my friends?" A sudden calmness came over me, all my anxiety draining into this new funnel of fury I'd never noticed before. "Damon." I walked over as Grace raced toward the door by us and bent down so my lips brushed his ear. I spoke, barely above a whisper, "*Vargulf Bentos Monstrum.* Hurt Grace or Michael, and I will bring a slew of terrifying issues which Grace and the Knightly family have no idea I know." I patted him on the shoulder and I straightened.

He turned completely white, then green. I stepped back, horrified at what I'd just done and worried he'd hurl his lunch all over me. His eyes grew huge and then darkened as they focused in on me. I had no idea what *Vargulf Bentos Monstrum* even meant. It'd just popped into my head. I remembered seeing the drawing in the journal with those words in a caption underneath. I probably hadn't even pronounced it correctly. The only thing I was sure of – I had hit a nerve inside Damon.

He snarled, "Kiss my a—"

"Is there a problem?" Grace's voice came out sweet but her body looked ready to pounce. She stood, legs slightly bent and on the balls of her feet. She grabbed my sleeve and held on firmly.

"No problem." I jerked my head in the mongrel's direction. "I think the cafeteria food's done a number to Damon."

Damon swallowed, his Adam's apple bobbing. "Rouge, you need to ask your friend how she, and the rest of her freakin' family, uses people to get what *they* want. Ask yourself if they really are the good guys."

"Go screw –"

Grace's warm hand squeezed my forearm, it stopped me. Her fingers grew hotter against my skin. "Let it go," she said quietly, her eyes never leaving Damon.

He scoffed and raised his arms, clasping his fingers behind his head. "Yeah, don't dig too deep, Rouge. You might not like what you see."

"Shut up Damon." Grace dragged me away, her lips pressed tight. "What'd you say to him?" She hissed outside in the hall.

"I just pretended to threaten him." I swallowed, suddenly feeling the urge to stare at my shoes. "I think you better get a hold of Michael. You might as well tell him to get Seth or however you guys handle these situations." My left leg started trembling. "I've a terrible feeling I just opened a can of worms."

"What did you say?" she repeated.

Chapter 8

"What did you say?" Grace asked again, shaking my arm.

I hesitated. *Lie or tell the truth? What had Damon meant about the digging to deep? Michael and Grace were the good guys.* "I repeated something from the Grollic book." I stomped my foot. "I'm such an idiot!"

Grace blew her bangs out of her face and shook her head sympathetically. "Damon's not going to run. They never do – until it's too late. I'd be willing to bet he's planning on watching you like a hawk for the rest of the day." The buzzer sounded to end lunch. "Our safest thing at the moment is to get to our next class. Damon won't do anything in front of everybody here. I'm not scared of that loser. I'll give Michael a heads up and he can meet us here at the end of the day."

I whispered, feeling panic welling up inside, "He knows what you guys are, and I'm ninety-nine per cent positive he knows we know what he is." I suddenly wasn't looking forward to the end of the day. Michael wouldn't be too happy. I wasn't completely sure what I'd done, but the anger I had towards Damon at that moment had taken over proper reason.

After last class, Michael waited by his Mustang which sat parked beside Grace's car. Seth stood at his side. Both in long-sleeve tops, but no coats, oblivious to the snow falling lightly around them. I'd kill for some of their natural body heat.

Every girl who walked by them slowed their pace and stared. Crossing my arms with my fists clenched under my armpits, I tried not to watch but couldn't stop myself. A girl would walk out of the school and veer in their direction, as if being called over or simply wanted to get a closer look. At a moment like this, I had time to be jealous of girls checking Michael out? I had just ruined everything by blurting out the one thing I should have kept quiet, and that was my problem? *I'm completely screwed in the head.* Then it hit me. *It's Seth they're googling over.* A senior group of females pushed past me, all fixing their hair or clothes, and half of them sucking in their bellies and adding a swing to the hips. I grinned and relaxed—for a moment.

I followed behind them, stopping in front of Michael and grew annoyed as the girls slowly trudged past. Finally out of ear shot, I crossed my arms and rolled my eyes. "Seth, do you have this problem everywhere you go?"

"Problem?" His eyes continued to follow the group. "I'm the luckiest man in the world. So many women and I've got so much time." He sighed happily.

"Dude! Pay attention." Michael sounded like Caleb as he spoke, aside from the dude-part.

Seth straightened. "I can multitask, you know. It takes so little to catch the young ones. I expend no effort." He coughed when Grace slipped soundlessly from behind me and punched him in the gut.

"Michael fill you in?" Grace asked. "What's happening?"

"Damon's not here," Seth answered, still clutching his belly.

"You sure? His car is."

Michael leaned forward, his arm coming around my shoulders. "If he leaves out back, Tatianna's there waiting."

Seth rested his elbow on the top of the Mustang and leaned back. Cold puffs of smoke escaped his lips as he spoke. "He's got to have just gone through the change so there's no way he's able to control it. There's no way a Grollic's going to walk by four of us and not try and attack. He's going to feel threatened."

"Three of us." Michael retorted.

"What?" Seth's eyebrows shot up. "Oh yea, three. Sorry. I keep forgetting Rouge's not one of us yet. When she dies and comes back, you'd better make sure you have her Siorghra, or you'll be killing off a few of your own kind, my friend."

Pounding exploded inside my ears. Did he mean Michael'll kill his own kind because the Coven would be mad? Or something else? With a stutter of hope inside, I wondered why he seemed so sure I was one of them. I tried to speak but my mouth had gone dry. I tried swallowing instead.

"Shut up." Michael pulled me closer to him. "Unless you have some information that's pertinent?"

Seth stared wide-eyed and gave a slight shake of his head. I didn't miss the grin he tried to hide.

"Maybe Damon left earlier?" Grace glanced at Michael and then turned to Seth. "I didn't watch him. I figured he'd be calling his gang to meet up here for an after school fight."

"Grace." Michael shook his head.

"He's definitely gone," Seth glanced up from reading his phone. "Tat's been inside the school. He's not here."

"What now?" I asked.

"Tatiana's going to try tracking him. If anyone, she'll find out where he's gone."

"Alone?" I asked. I might not like the girl but that seemed reckless to me. "Shouldn't one of you... be with her? What happens if a pack of Grollics attack?"

Seth chuckled. "Tat' can hold her own. She won't get caught. They'll never know she's been near them."

Grace slipped her backpack off her shoulder and brushed the fallen snow off Seth's hair. "Rouge *really* scared Damon at lunch. I've seen him angry but never spooked."

"Yeah, I got the picture from your message." Michael opened the passenger side door of the Mustang. "Seth, why don't you ride with Grace and I'll take Rouge."

It wasn't a question and again, his tone reminded me of Caleb. I slipped inside, happy for the warm heat. I sat quiet watching the world from my passenger window as we pulled out of the parking lot and drove down the street. Recalling what happened at lunch I blurted, "I royally screwed up today. Damon...He just made me so mad. I couldn't... I didn't think... I just reacted. I'm sorry, Michael. If Caleb didn't like me before, he's definitely going to hate me now!" I dropped my forehead against the cool glass of the window.

Michael squeezed my knee, keeping his hand there. "Damon already knows about us, and nothing you could have done will speed things up or change things."

"I wouldn't be too sure." Shaking my head, I closed my eyes and repeated what I'd said to Damon. It seemed like my lips were brushing against the skin of his ear again. "*Vargulf Bentos Monstrum.*" I blinked, forcing myself to focus on the picturesque view outside the Mustang. I just saw blurs of winter colors pass by. I had to tell him what I'd done. "I read the words in the Grollic book, but have no idea if I said them correctly or even what they mean." Deep down I knew I'd pronounced them exactly right. I wasn't about to admit that to anyone. "There was a picture in the book. It could be someone specific or just a drawing. I don't have a clue what and I'm an idiot for trying to scare Damon." I sighed and shook my head. "It was from a part of the book I can't even read."

Michael shrugged his shoulders. "I don't know the saying. Never heard it."

"Whatever it is, I scared the crap out of him and now he's furious."

"Vagif Ben—?"

"*Var-gulf Ben-tos Mon-strum.*" I repeated slowly. I scratched my knee, trying to remember what I'd found by Googling it. "It's Greek, or something."

"I don't know the Vargulf-part. However, Bentos sounds familiar but I don't know how." Michael put the car in park and sat quiet for a few minutes. He seemed to be focusing on his breathing. Long and slow breaths in and out.

We had already pulled into the driveway of the house. "Do we have to talk to Caleb right away?" I assumed that was his plan.

"Hmmm? Nah, we can chill for a bit. There's nothing Caleb and I haven't already discussed. Tatiana probably won't be back for another hour. Hopefully she'll have some information. I'd like to know if Damon's alone or actually spoke the truth and there are more." Michael stared vacantly out the window, his palm trailing back and forth over the top of the steering wheel.

He seems distant. I didn't know how to approach or help. I took my time getting out of the car and waited for him by the bumper.

Hand in hand, we quietly walked around to the pool house. I changed and started making dinner. Michael turned on the gas fireplace, sat at the bar while I cooked. He grabbed my laptop.

Exasperated, he shut the laptop and put it on the coffee table. "It is no use. I can't translate what the words mean."

"You said *Bentos* sounded familiar – maybe Seth or Caleb know more. We can head over to the house and ask. I'm just about finished sup—"

"Let's go." Michael stood at the door, already pulling it open, before I had a chance to set the spaghetti on the table.

With no one in the kitchen, we walked straight into the office. Caleb sat at his desk talking to Seth, who stood leaning against a book case beside the desk. Sarah and Grace sat in the red chairs, both upright and listening to the men argue. Conversation stopped when we entered.

"No news from Tatiana?" Michael asked.

"Nothing. However, she's not back yet, so that's a good sign," Seth replied.

Everyone turned expectantly to me. *What I'd do now?* I glanced at Michael in confusion. He leaned his head toward me and whispered, "They want to know what happened today, from your point of view."

I coughed and cleared my throat. "I got mad at Damon and didn't think."

"Should we be surprised?" Caleb snarled. "You didn't tell him about the book?"

I might be stupid but I'm not an idiot. "No, I didn't mention the book. I might've let on that I knew what he is." I took a deep breath and waited for the yelling to begin.

Except it grew quiet instead. No one said a word. I glanced around the room, settling lastly on Caleb. He'd be the most ticked. However, when our eyes met, there was no anger but something else. *Maybe a hint of respect?*

"What did you say to him?" His voice came out quiet, but direct.

"*Vargulf Bentos Monstrum.*" I stared at my hands. "I don't know what it means, just read it in the Grollic book. Do any of you know? I'm not sure if I'm actually saying it correctly." Again I felt this strange tug inside that it was exactly right.

"Monstrum must be monster or beast. What we used to refer to the Grollics as." Caleb's brows came together. "It was one of the terms we used in the very beginning. I do not know the other words."

"*Vargulf* means servant," Sarah said quietly. No one questioned why she knew, but I did turn to Michael and Grace for some sort of explanation.

"I was a warrior fighter a lifetime ago." Sarah sighed. "A hunter and fighter. That's how I found Grace and Michael." She smiled at them. "They are also the reason I stopped." She paced, her arms clasped tight behind her back. "My last orders were to hunt a pack of Grollics with a unique leader. He turned the Grollics into servants. We called them Vargulf Monstrums."

I wanted to ask what made her stop hunting the Grollics when she found Grace and Michael. Opening my mouth to ask, I paused when I saw the horror on Michael's face. "What's wrong?"

Everyone turned to stare.

His tanned face went three shades lighter, and his eyes turned sapphire blue. I stepped back without even thinking. He exhaled a terrifying growl as his head snapped toward Grace.

Her eyes grew big but the shock quickly turned to anger, her eyes turning the same ice blue as well. "No! How do you know?"

Michael's jaw clenched. "I remember everything from that night. It's imprinted in my memory like a movie. Earlier today...I thought...but it didn't..." He seemed to be sending messages to Grace and speaking only parts out loud.

Earlier, in the car he'd seemed distant. *Had he made some connection then? Or could he have been thinking about something else?* Now the shock couldn't be more genuine. I rubbed my neck, unsure of my own thoughts and wondering what the connection actually could be.

Caleb shouted. "What the hell's going on?"

Michael didn't take his eyes off Grace. "Bentos is the man who came that night with the Grollics. He killed our parents and then went after us. I don't know if he was a Grollic, but he lead the beasts. He's the one who stabbed me...tortured a-and r-raped Grace before he killed her. *Bentos.*"

I reached for his hand. He squeezed mine but then let go and turned to Caleb. "I think Rouge's uncovered a hidden secret." He looked at Sarah.

"I know very little, Michael." She came over to him and touched his face. "We'd been tracking and hunting that pack for months. We believed their leader had gone mad. We knew they were different than typical packs. The mess they made appeared targeted at certain people. Each death maliciously planned out." Sarah exhaled a long, slow breath. "That night they came to your house was the closest we'd been to catching them. They went underground right after, or got smart and cleaned up their act. My life changed, and I stopped my military crusades." She walked over to Grace and hugged her close. "My life had new meaning with the two of you."

Caleb coughed. "So is this *Bentos* an enemy to us or the Grollics – or both? Is it possible Rouge scared Damon with his name?" Caleb sounded all business, not one ounce of sentiment inside of him.

"I've heard stories but assumed they were tales," Seth said. "The man was human, so he can't be alive now. Right?"

I glanced at him in surprise. I'd forgotten he was still in the room. "The pictures and name came from a part of the book which isn't in English."

Caleb snapped. "I suggest you and Michael head to the pool house and get back to the book. There may be pertinent information we need. Have Michael look at the drawings."

"They weren't specific. I doubt they were actually of Bento—"

"I found them!" Tatiana burst through the door. Her hair wild and clothes a mess, but she appeared triumphant. She went straight to Seth, kissing him so passionately I had to look away, embarrassed. She finally pulled away and spoke to Caleb.

"Damon's merely a boy. Barely changed, maybe this past summer. He's a cocky uncut. There are nine in the pack, two older, plus a possible Alpha. The rest are young and want to fight. All full of stupid pride. Easy prey." She nodded in my direction. "After her challenge at lunch, Damon went running with his tail between his legs trying to find his Alpha. They're all terrified of the girl now." She laughed.

"Did they see you?" Seth asked.

"Didn't even realize I was there." She wiped her lips. "There were ten, but I had a little fun with one." She smiled dangerously at Seth and looked ready to pounce on him, her eyes shifting through different shades of blue.

"Focus, Tatianna. Where are they staying?" Caleb snapped his fingers.

"By a park, so I don't know where they live." She elbowed Seth. "Dummies. Too stupid to realize how dangerous being out in the open is. A bloody city park."

"Or bold and fearless knowing we won't do anything in broad daylight, in the wide open," Grace muttered.

I couldn't believe it. "They met as Grollics right out in the open?"

Tatiana snorted and Caleb shook his head. "Of course not." He glanced over me to Seth. "Do you see what I have to put with?"

"Watch it," Michael warned.

I hadn't thought the question was that stupid. *The way they talk...*

"What else did you learn?" Caleb ignored Michael.

"That's it. I scouted and counted. Then eliminated one. Now I want my prize." Her attention went back to Seth and she started to pull him toward the door.

"I don't think we'll be much help here for the rest of the evening, Caleb," Seth said with a sly smile. "I best take care of my mate before she causes any damage to your house."

You have got to be kidding me. I blinked and rolled my eyes at Michael.

"Go." Caleb flicked his fingers as if shooing a fly away.

Michael punched a fist into his other hand. "Grace, I don't want you or Rouge going to school."

"Fine..." Grace paused. When Caleb clear his throat she spoke again, "We're still celebrating Rouge's birthday on Friday. Even if it's just dinner, here at the house."

"No party, just us." Michael took my hand.

"I don't want to celebrate my birthday." I shook my head. "Now isn't the time. It's not important."

"I ordered cake." Grace crossed her arms over her chest. "You're blowing out candles."

Nobody argued. Michael and I left the office and walked out into the cold night air. The moon danced high in the clear sky, not quite full but its light giving an eerie glow among the trees and bushes – everything seemed blue tonight. *Something isn't right.* My gut seemed to be trying to convince my brain. I moved closer to Michael and he pulled me tight against him. Neither of us spoke as we headed to the pool house.

Chapter 9

Michael and I planned to work on the Grollic book late into the night, but ten minutes into it, I couldn't keep my eyes open. Despite all the worry and things learned, I needed to sleep. *Nice girlfriend,* I sarcastically thought as I drifted off.

I woke early the next morning with Michael missing and the room quiet. My laptop sat open on the coffee table facing me. I leaned over and ran my finger over the mouse pad. The screen flashed white with a note in the middle from Michael.

Gone to the house to speak to Caleb to see if there's any new information. I'll tell everyone to leave you alone. Relax and don't worry. You deserve a little break.

I showered, and then made breakfast. Sitting down on the couch, I opened the journal to the middle section by the Grollic anatomy. As I turned the thick pages, my nail caught a corner. Two pages were stuck together which I hadn't noticed before. I gently tried to separate and blew on them, managing to pry them apart.

My heart stuttered as I stared at the unseen pages. The words were in English.

Both sheets covered possibly vulnerabilities of the Grollic. I grabbed a pen to make notes on half used pieces of paper.

There was no hierarchy to the list - nothing to show the most or the least effective. Or what might not work. The points looked exactly like someone had jotted them down as they brainstormed. Nothing looked like it would work. They all looked ancient. Science had come a long way since this journal had been written.

I blew my bangs off my forehead. *So much for Hollywood and the movies they sell. Isn't there always a way to stop the bad guys?*

The point mentioned rye acting as another danger for the Grollic. There was a question mark beside rye-root. *Rye?* Wasn't that alcohol? Could whiskey do the same thing?

Useless," I muttered, tossing the pen onto the table. How's it gonna help if a Grollic's about to attack? Do I politely offer it a nice rye and ginger?"

The next indented notation in the book answered my question. A Grollic in human-form would be unable to shape-shift if it ingested rye. It could take hours to days for the rye to clear the body's system, which would leave the Grollic vulnerable in human-form.

Now this information might be important. I'd have to let Michael and the others know. If they didn't already know. After Caleb's comments last night, I wasn't too eager to share anything that wasn't solid. Glancing at the dull skies outside, I figured I might as well read the other page before heading over to share alcoholic possibilities which Caleb probably already knew and would only roll his eyes at me for sharing.

The next page talked about Alpha and Beta stuff. *Kinda like werewolves in movies.* I stood and began pacing the room. I needed to stretch and reading aloud might make better sense of the writing.

In a pack of Grollics, there is the Alpha, the leader, and the Beta, which are under the Alpha. Betas follow the Alpha till death. They do anything and everything they can to please their leader. There was no free choice once you became a Beta; you served the Alpha till death. A slave to its own kind." There was another note at the bottom of the page, messy and jotted down like an afterthought. It went along the bottom to the side edge since there was no room left. I couldn't make it out, only something that looked like:"Be the ultimate alpha.

Hello." Michael stood right beside me.

I jumped about three feet in the air, tossing the journal over my head. I hadn't heard him or the door open, hadn't even felt the cool air, till now. I shivered.

He caught the journal and handed it back to me. Sorry to scare you." He laughed and dropped down, pulling me with him. He let out a deep sigh, resting his arm on the back of the couch behind me.

Any news at the house?" I tossed the journal on the table, then snuggled closer to his warmth.

Nothing. Seth and Tatiana found nothing new this morning. No reports. Nothing out of the ordinary. It is just ... silent."

Maybe they left." I couldn't keep the hopeful sound out of my voice.

No, it's too quiet. Like the calm before a storm." He rubbed his forehead with one hand. Something's going to happen. We just need to figure out what."

What does Caleb think?"

He wants to wait a few days before he calls a meeting with the Higher Coven. He plans to flush the Grollics out." Michael scoffed; irritated by something I knew nothing about. He's sometimes like the beasts we chase. He acts as if this is his territory, like he's marked the trees. It's probably a good thing you were here. It's a bit of a mess at the house."

Oh no, what'd he do?" For someone high and mighty, Caleb had a lot of temper tantrums.

Living room's been re-arranged. No structural damage, but we do need a new couch and a few other pieces of furniture."

Do you all have these anger issues? Should I make sure and keep a lock on the door, so you won't ruin the pool house? It's kinda like the first place that's starting to feel a tiny bit like a home."

Michael laughed. You're safe, and trust me, a lock would be useless. Caleb's different. He needs his release and that's how he controls his fury. Better to destroy furniture than go looking for a fight with a human, when the Grollics cannot be found."

Wait a minute." My heart pounded in my ears. Why would Caleb attack a person?"

Ever seen a drunk guy try and pick a fight? Doesn't matter what you say to the guy or what you do, he's gonna find someone to take his pent-up issues out on. Caleb's a bit like that. He doesn't go trying to kill anyone. He just goes looking for a fight. With the biggest, baddest dude he can find."

I nodded. I understood what Michael was trying to explain, but it still didn't justify Caleb's actions.

Michael clapped his hands and sat up. Enough with the sludge of my day. Did you learn anything new from the book?"

I grabbed my notepad and slid the two ripped pages I'd just notes on at the back of the book, then flipped back a couple of pages. I did find something kinda cool. There were two pages stuck together which I hadn't noticed before. I found some information about Grollics vulnerabilities. You probably know all it already."

What we know we learned from battle. There's no manual and they're hard as heck to kill."

You're going to be disappointed then. Nothing really stuck out." I turned the page. There's something about rye but it didn't make any sense...kinda like someone wrote it as a possibility and never did the research."

Rye? Like the bread?" He scrunched his face. I don't think asking a Grollic if he wants a sandwich is going to stop him."

I giggled. And here I thought offering him a nice drink on the rocks might do the trick."

Michael smiled. Let's skip the scientific studies on rye and focus on what we do know. Caleb's been working on creating a weapon. Nothing has worked as of yet. If we can slow them down, there has to be a way to stop them.

We continued discussing the book. While I made some food ready, Michael jumped in the shower. After, he sat in front of the fire looking over maps of the area. He was determined the map would tell him where the Grollics camped. I set a plate by him and settled on a bar stool. I ate my sandwich and watched him mark off areas with circles, crossing off other spots.

I'm going to have Seth and Tatiana scout those areas." He pointed to an area marked with an X". That's where they've already been. They don't know the surrounding area and mountains as well as we do. I'd go, but Caleb has other plans." He crushed his fingers through his hair.

He needed a break. So did I. Want to take a walk outside?" I asked. I need a bit of fresh air. I've been cooped up in the cottage for most of the day and figure ten minutes of cool winter air might make my brain fresh again."

We should go buy you boots."

I'd completely forgotten with everything that happened yesterday. You sound like a mother-hen. All worried about my toes." I wiggled them at him to push my point.

I wonder what Caleb would think about that! I'm his understudy and next in line to the throne of the Higher Coven, and you call me a *mother-hen*." He chuckled, grabbing my toes and squeezing them. This little piggy went to market..." He pretended to bite it. What will my friends think?"

I didn't know you had any."

I do. Loads and loads, too many to count." He started rubbing my feet. Actually, you'll have to meet Tye one day. He's an understudy as well. You'll like him."

Is he Seth's understudy?"

No. Seth's understudy is just like him, except blond. He's the same with women as Seth. Disgustingly similar."

Don't let Grace meet him."

Why?"

I don't want her mated with some male harlot."

A deep snigger erupted from Michael. Gotchya."

Don't laugh. How're you going to feel when Grace comes home crying because she's mated to someone like Seth?" I shook my head. He cheats on Tatiana, you know? I don't know how she puts up with it."

Has he tried something on you?" The smirk disappeared.

Not with me. He just is... I don't even know what word to use... he definitely isn't the monogamous type."

Michael sat back. Neither is Tatiana."

I bet she would be if he canned his flirting act."

They're both players. She bates and plays just like him. They even have competitions against each other."

What?" I threw my hands up in the air. Just keep Grace away from his understudy. That's whacked."

Point noted. Just so you know our Siorghra doesn't work like that. You...You can't just give it to a total stranger and expect there to be a link. It can't be forced." Michael checked his watch. We'll have to shorten our outdoor time into a walk to the back door of the house. They're waiting for us, according to Grace. Caleb just wanted to see if you figured anything else from the book. Shall we go?"

Inside the big house, I peaked around the living room. Most of the furniture was gone, the carpet had fresh vacuum lines on it, and a fresh, clean smell filled the air. I poked Michael and started to giggle. He put his fingers to his lips and shook his head. Sobering, I nodded. It may be funny, but I wasn't about to push my luck and laugh at Caleb to his face.

Caleb, Sarah, and Grace were sitting in the office, talking quietly. Out of the corner of my eye, I checked Caleb. He sat typing something on a laptop, reading glasses on the tip of his nose. He appeared calm and relaxed. The living room episode erased from the room and him as well.

Are Seth and Tatiana coming tonight?" Michael asked.

If I need them." Caleb closed the laptop, his lips pressed in a tight line.

If Tatiana's right and these Grollics are just a bunch of rogues, they've no idea who they're up against. This'll be over before it begins," Sarah said.

Possibly, but there's something unique with this pack. They are all secretive. How is it we were unable to find them quicker? This has never been a problem before. We've been here three years and Grace says Damon has been here since she started school."

Young Grollics are dense," Sarah said. Maybe they knew nothing and only began making mistakes when they found us out."

Like approaching a human and pretty much telling her what we are?" Michael shook his head. Damon's made all the proper mistakes of a newborn Grollic... and an idiot."

Caleb scoffed. Stop acting like a love-sick boy. Use your head and start thinking properly."

Michael's shouldered stiffened. He walked toward Caleb. What bothers you? That the Grollics are planning an attack and we didn't realize? Or that they might not be chasing you? That's obvious. If they were after you, they would've attacked your labs or offices or something related to you. No young pack would come after you unless they had a death wish. Even the young ones know they don't stand a chance against the mighty Caleb."

Caleb stood and kicked his chair with the back of his foot in one motion. It crashed against the wall behind him and smashed into pieces. The rip of the leather and shattering of wood made me jump. Just barely fast enough. I dove to the side, between the desk and another chair.

He sprang at Michael and lifted him by the throat midair. Both men's eyes burned sapphire blue. Caleb threw Michael across the room as if he weighed nothing.

Michael hit a book case. The antique wood broke and books slid down the cracked shelves and tumbled onto the floor. Michael went instantly to his feet and fixed his shirt. He calmly walked back to where Caleb stood and held his hand up to stop Caleb from grabbing him again. Stop it! Are you angry with me, or the truth I'm spewing? We all know it's not about you this time." Michael glanced at me, Grace and then glared at Caleb. It has something to do with Grace and me."

Caleb threw his hands up in the air. Or possibly Rouge, an innocent girl who simply found a book by chance?"

My jaw dropped. *Me? Nah, impossible.*

Caleb snarled and pointed. Something about *her* is unsettling." He straightened, instantly calm. Do not risk everything you have for a mere child, Michael. It is unbecoming of you, and I expect a lot more. You are to lead this Coven one day. It is time you act as what you are —not some *weak being.*"

Michael jabbed a finger at Caleb. I know what I am and who I'm expected to become! I may be your understudy, but I AM NOT YOU. Don't ever take your frustrations out on me again. Next time, I'll fight back. That is something neither of us would want...especially you, old man." Michael's eyes changed to a darker shade of blue, but he appeared in full control of himself.

I blinked, realizing he was stronger than Caleb, in more ways than one. He purposely hadn't fought back.

No one said a word and no one breathed. The tension in the room was so thick I struggled to grasp the smallest of breaths to avoid passing out. I tried to inhale really quietly, but my heart was beating so fast I needed more air. Everyone's head swung in my direction as I gasped. I shrunk closer to the door and tried to steady my heart rate. Needing more, but embarrassed to make another noise I tried to inhale through my nose. I-I gotta g-go." I didn't want to be in this room any longer.

Without finishing, I darted out the office door. I kept my eyes on the floor and into the living room. Shivering and not moving fast enough, I couldn't get the image of Caleb's face so full of malice. I barged straight into someone heading toward the office. He grunted, stumbled and then dropped to the floor.

Seth.

I'm sor– " I stopped when I realized he didn't try to move. He just lay flat on his back. Holy crap," I whispered. Dark bruises covered his face, and a large cut on his forehead. His clothes had been clawed and everything he wore seemed deep red in color.

I gasped, not sure if the blood was his or someone else's. It seeped into the white carpet on the living room floor. I knelt down beside him and lifted his head in my lap. What the heck happened to you?" There was a gouge on his right shoulder where his shirt had been torn away. I put my hand against it to stop some of the bleeding. *Thank goodness I'd listened to a bit of first aid during class.*

Sw-wee...t-t-tiee..." Seth opened his eyes and stared unfocused at me.

His eyes were brown, not their usual bright blue color.

I did something I had never done in my entire life. I screamed.

Michael raced out of the office before my scream finished. He took one look at Seth and began shouting orders.

Sarah. Ice." He squatted down by Seth. Grace get gloves... for all of us." Sarah and Grace disappeared into the kitchen. The freezer door opened and frozen things crashed to the floor.

What's wrong?" I asked. He's hotter than boiling water."

Michael's head snapped in my direction. Rouge, get away from him RIGHT NOW!! If he's delirious he could kill you without realizing."

I fell back against the wall, too stunned to say or do anything else.

He's been bit." Michael's hand pressed against Seth's forehead. We're not going to be able to cool him off fast enough."

What happened?" Caleb rushed from his office.

Seth's been attacked." Sarah ran in with a pail of ice and dumped it onto Seth.

He jumped and tried to sit up. Tat...I'm not gone." He coughed, spitting blood onto the floor. Th-They came at us —"

Grace ran in with a pile of snow in her arms. She dumped it over Seth's head. The snow sizzled and popped as it melted at a rapid rate against his skin.

How's this going to help?" My whole body shook. Shouldn't we get him to a hospital or call nine-one-one?"

No." Michael continued to pack ice and, using another pile of snow Grace had brought, he packed it around Seth. His body's fighting the poison on his skin."

Seth struggled to sit up, only to be pushed back down by Caleb's boot. I-I've n-n-not been b-bit," he stuttered, his voice hoarse and cracked.

Michael," I whispered. His eyes..." I couldn't stop staring at their muddy brown color.

It'll be okay, Rouge," Michael whispered. Our eyes turn back to their natural color, when we're dying."

He's fighting it." Grace dumped more snow on him.

Caleb bent down and pulled back Seth's eyelid to show a blue pupil rolling left to right.

I dropped my gaze and stared at the wound on Seth's shoulder where I'd applied pressure. No blood seeped though, so I crawled closer to double check. His shirt was torn and soaked red, but no cut on his skin. I ran my hand over his shoulder and couldn't even find a scar. He coughed, making me jump.

Feeling better?" Michael sat down on the ground beside Seth.

Seth moaned and rolled to his side. I need a bloody drink. And a woman, maybe three."

You're definitely feeling better."

Caleb crouched down. Where's Tatiana?"

Seth pushed himself into a sitting position, his arms around his knees, fingers clasped. He said nothing for a long time. He heaved a deep sigh. Grollics attacked by the cabin. Surprised us. One went after Tatiana before we even had a chance to see the ambush. She got bit. Fatally." His head dropped between his knees. It happened so fast... I killed the bastard who got her, but they surrounded me after I threw him off."

Michael put his hand on Seth's shoulder.

The one who b-bit Tat... he went straight for her throat. She didn't even have time to pull him off. She didn't stand a chance." He shook his head. She's gone."

And the Grollic?" Caleb's foot tapped against the wet carpet.

Seth straightened. He wasn't the Alpha, but was one of the older ones. He didn't even seem surprised when I killed him. Like he knew he'd sacrificed himself. He kept mumbling that we had no idea." Seth closed his eyes, paused and opened them when he began speaking again. I'd have preferred to take my time with the bastard and thoroughly question him, but five more circled me."

I swallowed the lump in my throat. *Tatiana gone?* It just didn't seem possible.

Caleb, those boys know how to fight. They fight like in the olden days. No weapons —just brute strength and power."

Like in the beginning?" Caleb's brows rose high, his forehead showing wrinkles I'd never noticed before.

Yes! But most of them were young. Not long changed with raw strength, but old tactics. They were scared to bite me, afraid they might be infected, like they didn't know. That was my advantage and what kept me alive. They couldn't finish, and when I was bleeding so bad, they were scared to have my blood touch them. They figured I was pretty much dead so they took off."

Did you go after them?"

Seth stared at Caleb. No. I dragged my near-dead body back here so I could warn you. "

You were lucky then. What about the Alpha?"

I blinked in surprise. Caleb didn't rule with an iron fist, he had an iron heart.

No Alpha." Seth shook his head. He'd have known how to kill me. I think he sent the elder who I killed in his stead. Like I said, these are a new breed, they're young but different. With some new kind of knowledge from the old days." Seth slowly stood and looked to Caleb and then Michael. He reached into his pants pocket and pulled out two Siorghra necklaces. He separated them and stared at the one in his right hand for a long moment. He sighed long and sad, then tossed the one in his left hand to Caleb.

Keep that in a safe place for me. I'm not sure I'll need it again, but if I do, I'll know where to find it."

Caleb said nothing. He gave a curt nod and walked back into his office. Seth stared at the remaining Siorghra in his hand. Slowly he took the top off the pendant and closed his eyes as he drank the contents. He kissed the empty pendant. I'll miss you... He straightened and muttered, So much for being immortal." Making a fist around the Siorghra, he crushed the necklace into a fine powder in his bare hands.

Come." Sarah put her arm around his shoulder. Let's put the powder out in the wind."

Seth followed her and Grace out of the room to the front door.

Michael quietly walked over to me and held me tight. His warm lips grazed the top of my head. I leaned my body into his for support. It had been a crazy night —too much for my human eyes.

Chapter 10

Beams of sunlight poured through the windows, shooting tiny rainbows on every wall in the room. I stretched, my mood brightening at the sign of the sun that had been hiding for what seemed like forever. Sitting, the corners of my mouth pulled down at the amount of snow on the ground. *At least the new layer hides the dirty snow, and the bright blue sky meant the sun will do its job. It's going to be a good day.*

Michael stirred beside me and rolled so his head rested on my pillow and his body curved around me. My hand reached out to let my fingers sink into the thick blonde hair and enjoy its softness. He looked like his Greek god-self and I suddenly felt self-conscious. After raising himself up on an elbow, he leaned over and kissed me.

"Hmm. Mornin'." I couldn't stop my eyes from wandering down his bare torso – all that smooth, tanned skin over lean, taut muscles.

He raised an eyebrow and grinned. "Want me to put a shirt on?'

No! Maybe. "Do you need to head back to the house and check on Seth? I need a shower and grab breakfast. I can meet you over there.' I knew he had a lot on his mind, and I was sure he wanted to talk to Caleb.

"I can wait.' He looked like he meant what he said, but he also seemed like he wanted to go.

"Go. You don't need me tagging along.' I needed a bit of on-my-own time as well. "You must have important things to discuss. You're Caleb's understudy.' *Long before I even existed.* "He needs you.'

He sighed. "I guess you"re right. Caleb"s probably wearing a path in the carpet of his office. He was quite out of sorts last night.' He stood and strolled over to a duffle bag I hadn"t noticed laying by the bathroom.

"Does that... happen often?'

He shrugged. "Patience isn"t his strong point. I pushed the wrong buttons and I know better.' He disappeared into the bathroom.

I bit my tongue to hold back my thoughts. *You shouldn't be taking the blame. Caleb needs someone to put him in his place, and not just with words...* I blinked in surprise at my own thoughts, but couldn"t stop them. *And Michael's the only one who could do it.* I forced myself to sit and stare out the window, willing my brain to stop.

Ten minutes later, Michael came out of the bathroom dressed and with a quick peck to my cheek, he headed out the door.

The pool house felt suddenly empty with him gone, so I got up, made the bed and then hopped into the shower. I stood under the jet stream of hot water and closed my eyes.

How did Liza get the Grollic book? She"d closed shop and headed south for the winter so I"d get no answers from her till spring. Another thought bothered me about the book: why would Grollics write a book about their weakness, add anatomy and diagram it all? I couldn"t imagine Caleb having a book like this written on his kind. *If it ever fell into the wrong hands...* I shivered at the possible unknown danger Michael could become vulnerable to.

I grabbed the shower handle and slammed it off. *Too bad I can't read the rest of the book.* Maybe it would explained why or give more insight into who bloomin"wrote it.

I stepped out of the shower too frustrated to dry off properly or blow dry my hair. I dressed quickly and shoved my hair into a bun.

Michael must have come back while I was in the bathroom. By the door were a red winter coat and a quick scrawled note. *Grace found this in her closet. See you soon, M*

Outside, I zipped my new coat and followed a newly shovelled path, courtesy of Michael, to the house. Even with the sun shining, I had to pull my coat tightly around me and quicken my step. I should have gone back to the pool house to grab a hat to cover my wet head, but I couldn't be bothered. By the time I got to the back door, my hair had frozen in the bun.

As I stepped into the quiet, empty kitchen, I strained to catch any conversation going on in the living room. Nothing. They were probably all in the study. *Sound-proofing walls.* I hung my coat on the back of a chair and put my shoes beside Michael's. Grace appeared in the doorway, hands in the pockets of her jeans. Her green top seemed to make her eyes an even brighter blue.

"Want some coffee?' She walked toward the counter. "I think Michael just made a pot.'

I hesitated. "Umm... No thanks.'

She raised her eyebrows.

Ah, screw it. "Michael makes the most terrible coffee. It tastes like tar.' I grimaced still remembering the taste from the last time.

Grace tried to suppress a giggle but with no success. She went and got fresh coffee out of the cupboard. Without saying a word, she handed me the container and then emptied the three-quarter full pot into the sink, and refilled it with fresh water. "You know, Michael was a terrible cook when we were alive. My mother and I never let him in the kitchen. One year, he tried catching, killing and cooking a turkey for Easter.'

"I don't even want to imagine. Poor bird.'

"Poor us.' Grace grabbed her stomach and pretended to gag.

Glancing around the room, and leaning over to sneak a peek into the living room, I stopped short. "What happened?'

All the furniture had been pushed to one corner and stacked on top of each other. The original old pine boards reflected off the floor, emphasizing the missing white carpet.

"We couldn't get all of Seth's blood out, and it drove Sarah crazy. She pulled it up last night and left about half an hour ago to buy a new one. Knowing her, she'll haggle with some sales guy and have everything in before dinner.'

"How's Seth doing?' I kicked myself for not asking about him first.

"Physically he's completely fine. Like nothing happened. Emotionally, he's a mess without Tatiana, but you know how Seth acts... he keeps going on about being able to play the field and enjoy some – and multiple – female company for a change. Just his way of covering up, I guess. He mentioned his understudy may come down tomorrow after the meeting.'

"Meeting?'

"Sorry, I forgot you missed the rest of the conversation last night. The Higher Coven is meeting tomorrow to decide what to do with the Grollic situation here. Caleb wants things cleared up ASAP. Seth's considering bringing his understudy back here with him to help with the fight.' She swallowed, then stared at her fingernails. "Everyone's thinking the situation is bigger than we think, especially since they killed Tatiana and nearly got Seth.'

A fleeting thought of my birthday came and went. Eighteen had seemed so monumental to me, all my freedom wrapped in two digits. It didn't represent anything now.

As if reading my thoughts, Grace said, "They aren't leaving till noon. Your cake's still on.'

Mortified at the thought of Grace telling Michael, while Caleb stood in the room, about doing something for my birthday, I nearly bolted for the back door. "Please don't do anything. It's just another day, and honestly, I'm not big on birthdays.'

"Nonsense! You deserve a little celebration.'

"Please don't.'

She paused, a silly grin on her face. "I'll just tell Michael to make you breakfast in bed.'

"After the kind of cook you just told me he is? Great. The guy's probably going to squeeze the crap out of a chicken in order to get a few eggs to scramble.'

Seth came into the kitchen. "Fantastic morning, ladies! It's even lovelier now that you two have entertained my thoughts and given me something to feast upon!'

I looked up at the ceiling, trying to stop my eyes from rolling. *Definitely on the mend. Or in denial.* Tight black shirt with matching dark pants, there was no trace of injury on him.

Michael joined us in the kitchen. "I smell fresh coffee.'

Grace poured hot, black liquid into four mugs she'd lined up. "How about you tell us what the two of you and Caleb have decided?' She blocked the coffee with her arm. "Then you can have your mug.'

"Not much to say, really.' Michael shrugged, reaching over Grace's arm and picking up a mug. "We're meeting with the Higher Coven tomorrow afternoon. Seth thinks he can get rid of the Grollics himself. He feels Tatiana deserves that. Caleb believes there is something bigger going on than a bunch of young Grollics trying to pick a fight.'

I sat on a bar stool close by him and grabbed a mug. "What do you think?'

He held the cup to his lips but didn't drink. Finally he set it back down on the counter. "I think Caleb's right. Except I still don't believe they're after him.'

"You still think they're interested in us?' Grace asked.

"Why you two?' My heart beat thundered in my ears.

"I believe it has something to do with the night we lost our parents.'

"Why now? Wouldn't they have chased us down sooner?' Grace tapped her thumb against the rim of her mug.

"I'm not sure. It might have something to do with the book.'

"Maybe they're after Rouge,' Seth said from behind his mug.

My chair scraped the ground as I shifted. "I've got nothing, and until a few months ago I didn't even know they, or you, existed.'

"She's right,' Michael said. "She got the Grollic book by chance. Found it at a second hand shop. Caleb thinks they don't even know this book exists. On that count, I think he's right.'

"But still...' Seth persisted.

"Caleb did a background check on Rouge and nothing on the computer popped up that raised a flag of any kinds.' He touched my shoulder and squeezed it. "I just found this out this morning, myself.'

I wondered if Caleb had the name of my birth mother. As much as I wanted to know, I didn't ask. It wasn't the right time.

Michael shrugged. "At this moment, I'm not sure what to think.'

"Grollics always want to fight,' Grace said. "They don't need a reason.'

"True.' Seth strolled closer to her and reached around to grab a muffin. "But you'd be miserable, too, if you had all that testosterone and were ugly as dogs.'

"Seth!' Michael, Grace and I shouted at the same time.

Afternoon flew into evening and I found myself unable to stop yawning as the conversation floated around me in the living room. I sat at the end of the couch beside Michael, my toes squiggling into the new soft carpet Sarah had installed. Resting my elbow on the couch arm, I let my head drop into my hand. The conversation had quieted to a steady hum of male voices, becoming a lullaby to my ears.

I drifted and woke to someone gently shaking my shoulder.

"Rouge.' Michael's warm breath caressed my ear. "Let's get you to bed.' His arms slid under me and scooped me close against him.

I snuggled against his chest too tired to reply, until we were outside and cold crept up my back. *Freakin' freezing*! "Wha" the –' Twisting, I nearly fell out Michael's grip and into the snow, but he caught my flailing arm and leg.

A chuckle rumbled deep within his chest. "Relax. I'll put you in bed, safe and warm. Caleb still needs to talk. I'll be back as soon as I can.'

I nodded and once inside the pool house, easily drifted back to sleep. When I woke, the darkness had been replaced with early morning light. I knew right away I lay alone in bed. He'd probably ended up staying up to the wee hours with Caleb and Seth.

This sucks! Alone on my birthday.

As soon as the thought hit, guilt flooded though me. Michael needed to be with his family and he had a responsibility I knew so little about. Rolling onto my back, I sighed. What was Damon's comment the other day? I needed to figure out who the bad guys were? There wasn't an ounce of bad-stuff inside Michael or Grace. Now Caleb, he might be a different story.

Where could Michael be now? He had to see the Higher Coven in the afternoon so I'd hardly get to spend any time with him. Again the guilt washed over me. I wasn't that kind of person – the person who demanded they be shown love.

Disgusted in myself, I threw the covers off and stomped to the bathroom to shower. The hot water did nothing to ease my mood. I had a stiff neck, my shoulders burned, particularly the left side. I flipped the temperature as cool as I could take it, lasting another two minutes.

Hopping out and grabbing a towel to try and smother the goose bumps, I shook my head at the image in the mirror. "*Idiot*,' I mouthed.

I began towel drying my hair and decided to blow dry and straighten the mop – something I hadn't done in forever. Stretching to grab the dryer out of the drawer, I winced in pain. With my right hand, I reached behind to rub the soreness. However, the place couldn't have been in a more awkward spot. I looked like an ostrich trying to fly as I attempted to reach over my shoulder or around my back. I finally found an awkward, and slightly uncomfortable way by putting my right arm directly behind my back and flipping my wrist so my palm rested against my back.

I straightened when my fingers touched the spot. It was hot, burning hot. Twisting, I tried to find it in the mirror but saw nothing, just a small glimpse of my birthmark which looked slightly brighter than normal. I reached around again, but the area felt cooler, like typical skin temperature and the pain was gone. "Weird,' I muttered.

After blow drying and straightening my hair, I added eye shadow and mascara. Leaning toward the mirror, I paused and sniffed. *Bacon*.

Grabbing the spare jeans and top I kept in the towel cupboard, I dressed and peered around the door.

Michael's lean back and tight butt caught my attention. He stood scooping scrambled eggs onto a plate already heaped with bacon. He turned around, his shirt read: KISS THE COOK.

With a quirky smile, he looked up and sang, "Happy Birthday.'

I stepped out of the door and leaned against the wall.

Michael's eyes widened. "You. Are. Gorgeous.'

Suddenly it seemed like today was going to be the best day of my entire life. Whatever doubts I had when I woke now seemed silly and trivial. "Do I get to Kiss the Cook?'

"I hope so.' He walked over and kissed me with the softest lips in the world. He stopped before barely getting started. Taking my hand he set me on a bar stool.

"Did you make breakfast?' It smelled good, but Grace's warning on his cooking had me doubting.

"Of course! And not just any breakfast – bacon, sausage, eggs and toast!'

"Awesome!' I picked up a fork, eying the more black than brown toast.

He brought the plate over and set salt and pepper on the counter. Leaning onto his elbows across from me, he waited.

I pushed the first bite into my mouth and nodded. It actually tasted alright. *Maybe just a touch of pepper.* I dug in. No one had made me breakfast before and I wasn't about to ruin it. "What time did you finish last night?' I asked between mouthfuls.

"Just before dawn. I went to the corner shop to pick up this.' He pointed at the food. "Do you want to open your present now?'

"You didn't!' *Oh but you did!!* I was dying to know what he bought.

"Of course I did. So did Grace, Sarah... and Caleb.'

My mouth dropped in surprise.

"Who's do you want to open first?' Michael asked.

"I don't know.' I glanced around the room, trying to find gift wrapping. "Shouldn't we wait for the others?'

"Nah.' He grinned. "Grace insisted you open them on your own. She didn't want you to feel overwhelmed by everyone staring.' He tapped his temple and playfully rolled his eyes. "Pick a name.'

"Ummm... I don't know.' I ran my fingers through my straightened hair. "Wait. Save yours for last. Surprise me with the rest.'

He walked to the sink and opened the cupboard below. He pulled out a large rectangular box with a bag of black liquorice. "Grace's.'

I started to carefully peel away the tape then gave up and ripped it open. A large bottle of perfume. *Eternity.* "I'm going to pour this over her head.' I tried to sound mad, but couldn't hold back the laughter.

Michael handed me a small delicate looking box.

"This from Sarah?'

Michael shook his head. "Her gift is at the house.'

"You?'

"Caleb.'

"Oh.' Expecting a piece of jewelry, I lifted the lid and blinked. Inside laid a little radio, or some kind of iPod. Eyebrows raised, I turned to Michael.

He grinned. "Caleb thought you'd need a recording device to use while reading the Grollic book or if you had a thought or anything that might be of use. It records and you can hit the little orange button on the side and it'll transcribe your voice into an email that goes straight to your emails address—'

"And Caleb's?' I couldn't believe I'd thought it was a radio or some kind of iPod.

"Yeah.' He laughed, shaking his head. "He tends to be the impractical one.'

I tossed it onto the bed. "I'll be sure and record a thank-you on it for him.'

"Sarah also got you this.' He handed me another small box.

"I thought you said her gift was at the house.'

"It is...Open, and you'll see.'

I unwrapped. *A key.* For a car. "I can't accept this.'

He held his hands up. "Then you tell Sarah you don't want it. I'm not.'

Curiosity got the better of me. "What kind of car is it?'

"A surprise.' He smirked. "Want to go find out?'

"It's too much.' My mouth said the words but I was dying to find out what it looked like.

"Rouge, you plan on going to go to university next year. You'll need something to get back and forth.' He must've misunderstood the look on my face because he snorted and crossed his arms over his chest. "It's a bloody lease. You can buy it out if you want to after the three years are up.'

"Yeah, but...' I didn't know what to argue or say.

"You wanted eighteen to be big. Well, it is.' He checked his watch. "Is it okay if I give you my gift later? When I get back from the meeting?' His face gave nothing away.

"Sure.' *Is he... No...Maybe?* "Will it be just the two of us, uh, here?'

"I plan on it,' he whispered huskily, leaning forward and kissed me on the lips. I closed my eyes to enjoy the moment. When no kiss came, I opened one eye to peek at what he was doing.

He stood his head shaking and looking annoyed. "Fine. Grace is wondering if we're coming over to the house. She wants to know if you like her gift.'

"Is she a little persistent when you don't answer right away?'

"It's like she keeps knocking on the door. The door inside my head.'

"Let's go. I don't want you ending up with a headache. It's nearly one o'clock.' Michael would need to leave with Caleb and Seth shortly.

I stood and held out my hand. His warm fingers slid into mine as he kissed me on the mouth. This kiss was different; more passionate and wild. Whatever he felt made me want to hold him tight and not let go. Tempted to suggest we head across the room instead of out the door, I pressed closer. However, as impulsive as the kiss had started, he quickly pulled back.

"Sorry... gone all night, and now having to leave you this afternoon, I feel like I am going through a bit of Rouge-withdrawal.' He lightly traced the tip of my nose with his finger.

"I don't mind the needy kisses.' I giggled. One of those girlie laughs I'd made fun of all my life. I did one of those. "I'm happy to help take that feeling away.'

He groaned and pulled me into a tight hug. "You're going to drive me crazy. You already do and it can only get worse! A wonderful, intoxicating worse.'

"Well, if I'm the worst thing that's ever happened to you...'

"Come on.' He scooped me up. "Or I'll never make this Higher Coven meeting I already don't want to go to.'

Chapter 11

Michael held his hand out to let me step through the sliding doors first. A pyramid of birthday cupcakes sat on the counter. Flames danced on the number candles ' a one and an eight. Chocolate and vanilla cupcakes piled three high, each covered in whip cream and sparkles. Even though it was nothing big, it made my throat constrict. No one had ever bought, let alone baked me a cake. Not even Sally in the three years I'd live with them. *Uggh, after what she'd pulled why would I even think of her?*

Sarah and Grace stood behind the counter, looking like a couple of kids who couldn't wait to blow the candles out themselves. I smiled at their excitement. *Maybe this is kinda overdue for all of us.*

My heart melted. *How had I gotten so lucky?* I nearly stumbled as I realized how much I cared for all of them, not just Michael. Nothing in my life had led me to believe life should be like this. Yet, this all seemed... exactly right.

"Come blow out your candles!– Grace sounded like an excited six year old.

The kid inside of me ran over to the cupcakes, determined to blow them out before they did. I could forgive Grace's bottle of perfume ' for now. I pulled my hair back and blew lightly, paranoid I might let spittle escape at the same time.

"Happy birthday to you!– Grace and Sarah sang and clapped together.

My cheeks ached from all my smiling.

"Did you open up all your presents?–Grace asked, blinking and trying to look all doe-eyed.

"Almost.– Michael leaned over and grabbed a cupcake. "I'm going to make her wait till I get back from the meeting.–

Sarah walked around the counter and grabbed my hand. "Let's go see what's in the driveway.–She started pulling me toward the living room and front door.

I managed to grab an icing-loaded cupcake. "I...You...It's too much.–

"Nonsense! If you're going to be staying with us, you'll need a vehicle to get to school, hit the mall or wherever.–She paused at the door, one hand on the knob. "Ready? You go first.–She swung the door open, her eyes darting outside, to me, then outside again and back to me.

My jaw dropped. Beside Michael's mustang was a black Jeep. I didn't know what to say. How did one respond to the coolest, unbelievably expensive, awesome-ist thing in the entire world?

Sarah grabbed my hand again and pulled me towards the Jeep. "I thought about what you'd need. You're not like us. If you get stuck you'll need four-wheel drive to get out. I wanted something for you to feel safe in...and fun at the same time.–

"It's amazing...– Tears welled in my eyes, but I blinked them back. Girls who drive Jeeps don't cry.

"You like it?–

"I love it!– I ran my hand over the cold side and shivered. I needed a coat and also some mittens. "I can't wait to take it for a drive.–

"Let's go now!–Michael walked around to the passenger side.

"Michael,– Sarah spoke quiet, but with firmness I hadn't heard before. "You need to see Caleb. You're already running late.–

"I didn't forget.–He stared at Sarah with an unreadable face, and then turned to me, his brows popping up. "Let's get you inside.–He was at my side and put his arm across my shoulder, pulling me tight.

"It's too cold for you.–

I hadn't even realized my teeth were chattering, or I'd been shaking, till I felt the warmth he offered. Inside, I stood by the gas fireplace and held out my hands. Glancing around, I asked, "Where's Seth?–

Grace dropped onto the couch, licking icing off her fingers. "He left early this morning to set up for the meeting and check in with his understudy. He did say to tell you Happy Birthday. He offered to let me give you a kiss from him, and asked me to videotape it. Pretty as you are, I still refuse.–

"Totally fine with me.–I laughed.

Michael stiffened, his eyes darting to Caleb's office door.

A sinking feeling filled my stomach and I stared down at my half-eaten cupcake. "Time to head out?–

"Shortly,–Michael checked his watch. "Caleb needs to be there before everyone else. It's expected.–

"How long will you be?–

"Don't really know, to be honest.– Michael reached over and rubbed my cheek with his thumb. "Maybe a few hours. We need to come to a decision on how to handle the situation here.–

"Of course.–I nodded, but didn't get it. If Caleb, the highest and probably smartest dude in the group, and Michael, couldn't decide how to solve the problem how would anyone else?

Caleb strode out of the office, briefcase in hand. "Michael, let's go. The plane's ready, and I need to stop by the office downtown before we leave.–

Michael nodded. "I'll meet you by the car in a few minutes.–

Caleb grunted and continued to the front door.

It was hard to not stare. Caleb walked so regal and his entire being embodied strength. If the dictionary had pictures, his would be beside the world power.

Michael pulled me into a tight embrace. "Sorry to leave. I'd rather spend the day with you.–

I didn't mind, we'd be hanging out later tonight. "However, duty calls,–I joked.

Michael mock saluted in Caleb's direction. "I feel bad——

"I'll be fine. Go, before you tick Caleb off.–

He hugged me again and kissed the top of my head. He then put his hand on my chin and lifted my face toward his. He leaned forward, his lips tenderly touching mine.

"Happy eighteenth birthday, little Rouge Riding. I promise to give you my present as soon as I'm back.–

"I can't wait.–My mind raced with ideas. *Maybe I'll cook dinner for us.* "Wait. Did Caleb say he had a plane?–

"A small one here in town. And a little private airstrip.–Michael grinned.

He definitely was royalty. The guy probably had an Air Force One plane. "Where's the meeting?–

"On the East Coast.–

"I love you. Hurry home.–I blushed, the words out before I could stop them.

He smiled, big and goofy. "Love you, too. Stay safe.–He slowly let go of me and headed towards the front door.

His walk's similar to Caleb's. Funny, I'd never noticed. I gave him a small wave from the window and watched the car disappear down the drive. I stood there long after they had gone, my eyes travelling around the front yard. Then I had one of those thoughts that you wish you could take it away the moment it enters your mind. *What if this is the last time I see him?*

I shook my head, trying to erase the silly notion. But once those stupid thoughts were in, you couldn't get them out. I needed a distraction. My eyes settled straight in front of me. *Jeep.*

I could shop and make dinner for tonight.

"Grace, I'll be *fine*.–I rolled my eyes as she followed inches behind me to the Jeep. "It's groceries. I won't be long.–

"I trust you. Please don't think I don't. I just know what Michael's going to say when he finds out I let you go off on your own.–

"It's ten minutes down the road! What kind of trouble can I get into there? An old lady knocks me out with her cane 'cause I grab the best head of lettuce?–

"True...No Grollic's going to come after you in a crowd of people.–

"They aren't interested in me.–

"Why don't I come? I can just wait in the car while you shop.–

"And leave Sarah in the house alone? Would Caleb be alright with that?–With Sarah's military background, she's probably safer than the rest of us. "Michael's positive they are after you and him. You're safest place is here.–

She played with an earring. "Are you sure you'll be alright?–

"I just want to make dinner for Michael.–

"Ohhhh.–She grinned, punching my arm. "Now I get it. Why didn't you just say so?–She winked, then headed back inside. Then she popped her head out one more time. "Fifteen minutes. Twenty tops. Then I'm texting you and hunting you down myself.–

Shaking my head, I opened the Jeep door and sat on the tanned leather driver's seat. The "new– car scent teased my nostrils. Checking the wheel and dashboard, I finally found the ignition and started the engine. I pulled forward slowly trying to set the mirrors and realized the seat also had automatic adjustment. *This vehicle's cooler than cool.*

Flipping the radio on, I drove and turned carefully into the lot of the grocery store. Paranoid, I parked towards the back, far away from the other cars. As I dashed toward the store trying to avoid road salted puddles, fresh snow flakes started to fall.

I grabbed a shopping cart and made my way around the outside part of the grocery store. All the fresh produce sat on the outside aisles and the packaged goods were in the middle. In line for the checkout, I stared at my cart. Maybe I bought too much. I just wasn't sure if Michael liked chicken, hamburger or salmon. Setting my stuff on the counter, I saw a little rack with mini bottles of alcohol.

Glancing around and not seeing anyone I knew, I threw two rye ones with the rest of my groceries. Fingers crossed the cashier wouldn't ask for identification.

No luck.

"ID, please.–

I stared down at my wallet and handed him my licence, knowing full well I was screwed. *Stupid. Stupid idea.*

The check out guy, who didn't look much older than fifteen, checked the date, glanced at me, then down at my card again. Handing the card back, he tossed the bottles in my bags and never bothered to look up. "Happy Birthday.–

Stunned, I paid and left. *I'll pay it forward one day, kid.* Outside the snow had begun falling harder. Large, fat flakes sparkled as they drifted in the masses toward the ploughed parking lot, hiding the mud and salt. I shook my head, I still needed boots. *Tomorrow.*

My lovely, lonely Jeep waited patiently for me. I threw the bags into the backseat behind the driver's side and quickly hopped into my seat.

I leaned to pull my keys out of my coat pocket and nearly dropped them when the passenger door opened and someone hopped in.

I closed my eyes and took a deep breath. "Grace! I told you nothing would happ——– All conversation fell away when my lower left shoulder blade started to burn like fire and I caught a whiff of wet animal.

Damon.

Chapter 12

"So glad I found you." Damon's eyes were full of mockery.

"Get. Out." I pointed to the jeep door, and shifted trying to ease the sudden ache in my shoulder blade.

"No can do." He pointed his thumb to the exit. "Get this thing started and head onto the road. I'll tell you where to go."

I'd like to tell you where to go. "I'll leave, *after* you get out." Bile rose in the back of my throat. "I'm not taking you near Grace."

"Rouge, start the friggin' Jeep, or I'll start it for you. And you do *not* want that." He snarled. His eyes turned a terrible yellow color, the same shade that haunted my dreams.

Frozen, I tried to get my brain to process any coherent thought. Grace and Sarah wouldn't start to worry about my absence for another ten minutes. Michael and Caleb were gone, so I was pretty much on my own. Damon didn't know...He couldn't right? "M-Michael an-and Grace are meeting me here, any minute now."

His barking laugh reverberated off of my own chest. "Nice try," he spat, as if reading my thoughts. "Michael's halfway across the country and well, let's just say Grace and her dear so-called momma aren't going anywhere."

My shoulders and lungs dropped as if they'd collapsed. *The Grollics have Grace and Sarah?* They'd been waiting and watching till they were most vulnerable. "You'd better not hurt them," I hissed.

"We won't... for now. If you do as I say, it might be for a bit longer." He grinned. A stupid, irritating grin that made me want to tear his face off.

What choice did I have? "Fine. I'll drive. Just leave Grace and Sarah alone." The closest thing I had to a family wouldn't die if I could help it. Damon didn't need me. He just wanted to get to Michael and Grace. I knew he didn't stand a chance against Michael.

Damon raised his eyebrows for a quick second. "Good."

My hands shook as I turned the ignition and grasped the wheel. I leaned to turn up the heat, hoping it might give me some courage. Whatever I did might mean life or death for Grace and Sarah. If Grace contacted Michael through their ESP-thing, he and Caleb might be heading back. *Did the Grollics know of their ability?*

"Turn right out of the parking lot and head towards the highway. We need to get off at the exit before the lake." He sniffed and turned his head to the groceries in the backseat. Grabbing a bag of chips, he opened them and started eating. The idiot had the audacity to offer me some of *my* chips.

"No, *thanks.*" I focused on the road as the snow began falling in thicker, heavier flakes.

"Drive like you're going to the head to the Knightly's cabin. We'll park the Jeep there and head out again. We'll take your groceries along as it would be a shame to let all this good stuff go to waste." He turned and dug through the bags. "What's with all the healthy crap? You need more starchy foods. They fill you nicely." Damon patted his stomach, stuffing another handful of chips in his mouth.

I squeezed the steering wheel tighter, my knuckles white against the black leather. Like I cared about food groups at the moment. "I have no freakin' clue how to get there." I lifted my foot off the gas and let the Jeep slow its pace.

He grabbed my arm and squeezed. It hurt like crazy and if he tightened his grip a fraction my bones would break. "Listen closely as I'm only going to say this once. It's in your *best* interest you try and humor me. Keep me happy and content. I'm the only one who can save you." He swore under his breath and punched the dashboard. "Just drive and keep your mouth shut!"

I dropped my foot back on the gas pedal and pressed my lips tight. I rubbed my sore arm. If I ticked Damon off in the Jeep he might shift into a Grollic. What if he changed and bit me? *Could that make me a Grollic?* If that could happen, everything with Michael would be doomed, and I did not want to spend an eternity living without him. The Siorghra around my neck tingled against my skin giving me a small warning. Glancing around, I realized I didn't know where we were. I'd only been to the cabin once with Michael, and it had been dark. Blinking back the water filling my eyes, I whispered, "I don't know where I'm going."

"Take the third exit, and head north. I'll tell you where to turn when we get there." Damon went back to eating the bag of chips and began ignoring me.

Forty minutes later, with no decent plan popping into my head, I turned into the snow covered road which let to Caleb's cabin. Thank goodness for the Jeep's four wheel drive. Nothing had been cleared in days. No trace of the fight between Seth and Tatiana against the Grollics existed, except for the odd fallen tree and a large clawed gouge mark on a maple close to the cabin. My breath caught as I rolled to a stop and let the engine idle.

"Stay in the Jeep." Damon swung his door open. "Don't bother even thinking about taking off. We'd catch you on foot, or on wheels or with a bullet." He jumped out and jogged toward the tree line on the right. He whistled into the forest and leaned against a tree, his jacket open and oblivious to the cold.

A female, a couple years older than me, emerged from the trees. She walked to Damon and stood inches away from him, then began pulling the black hooded sweater off and he pulled at her belt.

"Great," I muttered, dropping my gaze to the crumpled bag and chip crumbs all over my passenger seat. "Just what I want to watch.

Two Grollics gettin' it on. Disgusting." I jumped at the sharp rap against the side window.

The passenger door opened and the girl dropped into the spot Damon had vacated. She began pulling off her boots. "Give me your clothes," She commanded in a husky voice.

I stared straight ahead, not moving.

"Get your crap off or I'll do it for you, bitch." Her husky voice turned into a growl as she grabbed my shoulder and squeezed hard.

"Ow! That hurts." Her sharp nails dug deep into my skin, even through my coat. The pressure didn't weaken. She could crush my bones if she wanted. I pressed my lips tight to cut off the groan trying to escape. She lessoned her grip when I reached for the hem of my coat. I lifted my elbow and pushed her arm away and then pulled the zipper down on my coat and shrugged it off. At least I didn't have to watch them messing around.

"Take everything off. Then put on what I'm wearing."

Silent, I did as she commanded. My thoughts kept drifting to Grace and Sarah, hoping they were safe. Whatever the Grollics plan was, they would take me to them, right?

I tossed my wet sneakers on her lap and had the satisfaction of watching her nose wrinkle. She kicked her boots on the floor by my feet. I snorted. *Finally got a pair of boots for the snow.*

I struggled to get dressed in the tight space under the wheel, but Damon's ugly face pressed against my window helped speed the process. The girl's clothes smelled damp and of wet fur.

"Perfect! And Damon said I was too big." She leaned forward, staring directly at him. With a grunt, she got out and walked to the front porch. The girl paused on the porch and played with her earring before dropping to sit on the steps, and rub her arm against the railing. After leaving her – my – sneakers at the door, she slipped her hand inside the sleeve of my sweater and wrapped it around the door handle before heading inside.

My breath sucked in sharply. *She's putting my scent around the cabin.* I wouldn't be staying. I tried to think of something I could do inside of the Jeep. A clue which might help Michael. Something to let him know it was a trap, and I wasn't inside the cabin.

Damon had stepped in front of the Jeep, hollering at the girl to hurry, then turned and glared at me. I touched Michael's pendant and ran it along the chain.

An idea skittered across my mind. I reached for the clasp at the back and pulled with both my hands. It unclipped easily. A little wave of disappointment flushed through. Michael had said no one could take it off if he put it on. *Shame he'd never get the chance.*

Swallowing the lump in my throat, I dropped the Siorghra on the floor, pushing it slightly under the seat.

Damon came around to the driver's side and wrenched open my door. He reached in to turn the ignition off and tossed the keys in the snow. Grabbing me by the collar, he dragged me out and then shoved me in the direction the girl had come from the forest.

"Walk," he barked, then swung around and grabbed the bags of groceries from the back seat of the Jeep.

The girl never came out of the cabin. I ran my fingers through my hair and scrunched my nose at the loose strands entangled in my fingers. I shook them out at the edge of the forest where we headed into the trees. Pushing me in front, Damon pointed the direction to walk.

I moved in front but glanced back at the cabin. The amount of snow in the forest was higher than I'd anticipated. "Where's Grace? Is she in there?"

"Shut up." Damon scowled.

"No. Where's Grace and Sarah?"

"Not right freakin' here."

I stopped, knee deep in a snow drift, and crossed my arms.

Wrong move.

He marched right up to me and, before I had a chance to flinch, curled his fingers around my throat. "Walk. Or someone's going to end up dead." He squeezed tighter, emphasizing his point.

Slapping and trying to pull his hand away, I struggled to get air into my throat. Little flecks of white danced in my vision and just as everything started to blur, he let go. I fell back into the soft, wet snow. Sucking in sweet, cold air against the burning in my throat, I rolled to my side.

Damon kicked my hip. "Get up."

Wiping the tears that had escaped my eyes, I managed to get onto all fours and slowly straighten to standing. Damon shot me a single nod and pointed. I dropped my head and started to walk, trying my best not to swallow.

We hiked for what seemed liked forever but when I checked my watch, only about forty minutes had passed. The soreness in my throat dulled, but there were going to be bruises. Though tired, I resisted the urge to ask Damon where we were going. I'd given him the silent treatment since the cabin. *Jerk. Big stinkin' dickhead.*

The grey snow clouds made the sky get darker earlier than usual. *Does he plan on walking all night, or worse, camp in the snow?* The loser may be a Grollic but I'd freeze to death. The snow hadn't stopped falling and had covered all our tracks. I grabbed my hair, wishing I'd left a ponytail holder around my wrist. I tugged a few strands out, trying to use them as a pony. *Useless.* They just drifted away or came loose.

Damon grabbed my arm and glared at me. My heart stuttered. I hadn't been paying attention to where I'd been going. A gouged out creek that ran into the lake had a small drop from years of water pushing through. One more step and I'd have fallen the three feet and crashed onto the ice.

His arm dragged me left. "Keep walking and frickin' pay attention to where you're going."

I wrenched my arm free and stomped through the heavy snow. Fifteen minutes later, I could just barely make out a dark outline through the early night shadows. As we came closer I realized it was another cabin – sort of similar to Caleb's but a lot older.

Damon, still carrying the grocery bags in one hand, grabbed my wrist and pulled me up the steps. I managed to grab the railing to stop from stumbling. He barged through the open door and dragged me, and the groceries, inside.

Flicking lights on, he said, "Put these in the kitchen and wait there." He stepped back outside.

I waited by the door, trying to stare into the darkness if I could make a run for it. A quiet howl erupted followed by two shorts barks. No way was I going to try running, or stand in front of the door. I grabbed the bags and strode down the little hall, through the living room to the kitchen.

Everything in the place was dated. Old cabinets, almond coloured stove and fridge that ran so loud, it made some of the cracked linoleum shake. I dropped the groceries on the counter and checked my watch. Almost seven.

The front door slammed. Damon walked in and took off his coat. He started emptying the bags. "Can you cook half decent?"

"Wuh – Wuh'ever," I replied, my voice hoarse. It hurt to talk.

"Cook everything. I'm starving." He sat back on a bar chair and crossed his arms over his massive chest.

"Excuse me?"

"Feed me, then we talk."

"Feed yourself," I mumbled. No way would I be his chef.

"Rouge...Don't. Piss. Me off," Damon hissed through gritted teeth. He jumped off the chair and sprang towards me.

I stepped back, but still tried my best to scowl at him. *You don't scare me by trying to act tough.* The hate for him, and those monsters swelled inside of me, making my shoulders ache. Especially the weird spot near my scapula.

Except it was different this time. Like the inside of my skin burned and the flame found its way into my veins and began to spread everywhere.

Damon growled in my direction, his eyes narrowed and turned a dark red, almost black color. His face twisted and his teeth grew, his mouth and nose elongated at the same time his chest cracked and expanded beyond what any normal human could live through. His back took on a kyphosis look and then arched jerkily. The black eyes burned to an amber colour. *Kinda like my eye color.* The thought slipped away as thick, matted hair covered his body and his skin thickened to gross dark leather across his chest. Within seconds, he'd shifted.

Time stopped. At least I swear it did. My blood forgot to flow, thunder erupted in my ears and my insides shook with horror. This *mammoth* creature was no Grollic from the journal. The thing stood on its rear hunches, its front legs appendages used as arms or legs. No horror movie would ever scare me again.

It looked like some kind of demonized animal. A low growl rumbled inside its chest. I froze, too terrified to even scream. The big bad wolf from Red Riding Hood had nothing on Damon.

It stared at me, then shifted its head to purposely look at the groceries. I understood and hesitantly took a tentative step toward the counter. *Either I cook or become dinner.* With shaking hands, I began separating vegetables and setting the meat by the stove. I didn't stand a chance and I doubted Michael would against a pack of these horrific creatures.

The beast spoke, its voice so evil it chilled me to the core. "Don't tick me off again. Make the food. All of it." Then it left the room.

Frozen, nothing inside me could move. Except my heart. It probably beat more in those moments than it had in its entire life.

Do something! My brain screamed. "What do I do?" I whispered back, unsure if I meant right now or in the bigger picture.

I turned the stove on and dumped the hamburger into a frying pan. I tried to cut the onion but my hand wouldn't stop shaking and I came close to chopping a fingertip off instead. Leaning against the counter I focused on slowing my racing heart, taking slow, deep breaths. Hands covering my face, I couldn't erase the horrific images glaring behind my eyelids, as if burned there forever.

Chapter 13

I shoved the chicken into the oven and kicked the stove door shut. Swearing under my breath, I dumped the cooked hamburger in with pasta I'd already bowled and then started frying an entire package of bacon. Somehow, without even realizing it, I'd made a salad and buttered an entire loaf of bread.

Pacing from the fridge to the stove, I tried to clear my head. I needed a plan, or something. I was terrified for Michael, Grace, and Sarah. Except not so much Caleb; he could handle his own. I hoped.

"Crap," I muttered, flipping the bacon over. "Here I'm freakin' cooking for the enemy." What could this useless human do against a pack of Grollics?

Damon strolled back into the kitchen, whistling some stupid, merry tune. He opened the fridge door. "Never anything to drink." At the sink, he poured himself a glass of tap water, downed it, and repeated filling his glass about ten times. He set the glass back down on the counter and turned to me.

"Did you buy any coke?"

"I don't drink –"

"Just shut up." He grabbed a plate and started tossing pasta on it. Dumping most of the bacon on top, he grunted when he noticed the salad. "Crap." Flipping the oven open, he sniffed loudly. "Good. You can do something right." He left the kitchen and shouted from the living room. "Make yourself a plate and get in here."

I stood debating. There was nowhere to escape from in the kitchen, and if I took a knife to attack him, I'd probably be the one who ended up with it in my heart. I could read a freakin' Grollic book and what good did it do? Filling a plate with salad and the rest of the bacon, I almost dropped it when I remembered the rye bottles. I had no idea if it would work, but if I could prevent Damon from turning into a Grollic, I might be able to get away. *Yeah, and then face who or whatever's outside.*

Searching the grocery bags, my throat tightened. Empty. *Did they fall out in the jeep? Please no!* A last bag lay crumpled on the counter. Already assuming the worst, the muffled "clinking" sounded like music to my ears.

With shaking hands, I poured the two bottles into one glass. Tempted to take a swig to calm my nerves, I resisted simply because I couldn't waste a drop if it might work. Holding the glass up, I frowned. It sure didn't fill a glass much. *Ice.*

I checked the freezer and fist pumped before grabbing a tray of ice cubes. Throwing three in the glass, I swirled the liquid with my finger and then buried the empty bottles in a drawer. Forcing myself to walk and act normal, I made my way to the living room, a small plan forming in my mind.

Damon sat on the couch, his plate already nearly empty. He glanced up and pointed towards the armchair beside the couch. I set the glass on the coffee table and sat down.

He snatched the glass and lifted it to his lips before I could even pretend to protest. Gone. In one gulp. He sputtered and shook his head. "What the hell was that?" He coughed and wiped his mouth with the back of his hand.

"A-Alcohol. I poured it to help calm me down." I swallowed, holding my plate with two hands so it wouldn't shake. "Guess it didn't help me much."

"Someone hid it here in the cabin? Figures. You couldn't handle the stuff, it's way too strong for you. Plus you're going to need your wits about you."

"Why?" I swallowed. Thank goodness he didn't ask if there was more. I relaxed a tiny little bit. He obviously knew nothing about rye. Either that or it was useless.

"You have no idea about any of this, do you?"

"Any of what?" I blinked focussing back on him. Maybe he did know about the rye and it was just folklore. I sighed. *Some freakin' birthday.*

"You really are an idiot." He shook his head and leaned forward, grabbing a piece of bread off my plate. "For starters, Grace and the other chick aren't here."

"Duh, I can see that." He was the idiot. "You've got them somewhere else."

"Nodda. We don't need them, or your precious Michael. I mean, shoot, we'd be glad to get rid of 'em, whatever cost, but we already have what we want."

They have Caleb?

"The bonus," he laughed, unable to continue and bits of soggy, chewed bread flew out of his mouth, "is that we'll use you to kill them off, as well."

I put my plate of food down, suddenly sick to my stomach. I asked the question though I was pretty sure I knew the answer, even if I had no clue as to why. "Who've you been after if it's not them?"

He leaned back stretching his arm along the back of the couch, a wicked grin on his face. "You."

Fear leapt into my throat, blocking my airway. I tried to swallow it back down. "Wh-What're you going to do? Bite me and turn me into a Grollic?" *So I can't be with Michael?* It didn't make sense. Nothing made any sense anymore.

Damon huffed. "Stupid girl. We don't reproduce by biting someone." He pulled the collar of his tee shirt, exposing his mark. "This is royal blood. You are born into this family, not made. We officially shift when we turn eighteen."

"What?" Nobody thought any of this might be important to explain to me? Either from the Knightly's or in the stupid Grollic book? I couldn't stand Damon, or any other Grollic. A sudden thought made my heart stutter, I was eighteen today. Did Damon know? Or, was it even important? It didn't matter, I didn't have the mark on my chest.

"Close your mouth, Rouge. Your new family failed to teach you our history?" He leaned forward. "I told you not to trust them. They're after you for the same reason we are."

"They've never been after me." I glared at him. "Except probably now they are, since you kidnapped me."

"I hope they are. You're our destructive weapon." His mouth curled into a snarl. "But, you have no idea about any of this, do you?"

Maybe the alcohol had gone to his brain. "I don't have a clue. Why don't you fill me in and quit being cryptic."

"Cryptic?" He cackled. "Let me start with this. Michael knows who you are, and once you're eighteen he's never going to want you back in his life." He let out a ferocious laugh.

My stomach clenched with dread. "What're you talking about? Wait...What did you mean when "I" turn eighteen?"

Damon crossed his arms and dropped his feet onto the couch. "Poor little orphan girl no one wanted. Did you ever wonder why your parents abandoned you? Or wonder who you were?" He laughed. "You'll never see your eighteenth birthday."

About to tell him I was already eighteen, I paused. Maybe keeping that quiet was the only advantage I had. "How do you know so much about my past?"

"Don't you know anything about your real parents?" He made a fist and punched his other hand. "I didn't clue in until that day in school when you said *Bentos*. Then I figured everything out, all by myself." His chest puffed out. "When the Knightly's moved here a few years back we knew they were after something. We just had to wait until it revealed itself. You gave away your secret so easily that day. It was like take candy from a baby."

He had no idea about the journal and I had no intention of letting on. "Bentos is just a name in my head."

"Of course it's in your head!" He leaned forward. "Do you know anything significant about it?"

No way would I admit I knew Bentos had killed Michael's family. My silence must have been an answer for Damon. "I don't know anything."

"Here's your history lesson and listen well, it's important. Bentos was the seventh son of a Grollic." He held up one hand and two fingers. "Remember that number. Seven. Way back, the seventh child of a Grollic was given the Christian name Benjamin or Bentos to protect him from becoming a Grollic. He'd be different and unable to join the pack. However, this one Bentos got pretty pissed off his family would be Grollics and he couldn't shift. So *this* Bentos, in anger, murdered his father."

I shifted, uncomfortable where this story might be going, and moving because my neck, back and shoulder blade ached. All of me did.

"Bentos' father was an Alpha and after he killed him, he figured out how to control his father's pack of Grollics. He could control any pack, even an Alpha. The seventh son with a special ability."

"What does this have to do with me?"

"I'm getting to that."

I stared dumbly at him. None of this made sense.

"A hundred and something-odd years ago, Bentos took a bunch of packs of Grollics and used them as if he were an Alpha. He controlled them, the paranoid dick-head. Had them prey on humans for money or women or whatever he wanted. He raped many women, bore children, and killed his offspring so they couldn't take his gift from him. He hated Grollics, but loved the power he had over them." Damon flexed his bicep, staring at the upper muscle in his arm. "You don't know this?"

I shook my head, too afraid to speak.

"This Bentos killed Michael's family. The story goes on that he'd seen Grace in town that day and wanted her. There was something weird about those twins back then. Bentos knew it. He had the Grollics attack at dusk, but the Fallen were in the forest nearby and interrupted."

"The Fallen?"

"Michael's kind. We call 'em Fallen. If you don't get why, figure that one out yourself."

I smiled as I realized Sarah must have been close on Bentos' heels.

"Your Fallen aren't going to want anything to do with you, dear Rouge. You're tainted, you're almost one of us." Laughter erupted from him, so loudly it made me jump. "Except to us, you're worse than a weak Grollic."

"Whatever. I'm not a Grollic. You're disgusting" I hated them, no freakin' way their blood ran in my veins.

Damon slapped my face hard. My head swung so fast to the right, I swore it cracked and adjusted every bone in my vertebrae.

"Get it through your head," he growled, "you are one of Bentos' offspring. *You* are the seventh generation and the seventh child. You, bitch, are the one thing *none* of us wants. No Grollic wants you and your new little family's going to let you rot when they learn the truth." He dropped down, his face inches from mine. "My only question is how Bentos didn't kill you off."

My cheek burned, but I refused to rub it. My childhood flooded back. No one had ever wanted me – even my own mother abandoned me. The euphoria I'd been feeling the past few weeks dissolved in an instant when I realized Damon was right.

What if Michael hated me? He'd have good reason. My father or ancestor killed his family, and I had the same blood running through me. I slumped against the back of the chair, suddenly exhausted. *Happy freakin' Birthday. Whahoo.* Could Michael already know?

"The truth hurts, doesn't it?" Damon's hands grabbed the end of the arms on my chair and tilted it back. "Or, maybe it's the realization you knew all along."

I stared at him, wide eyed. Here I'd been hoping I had the same blood of Michael's running through me. That I'd be part Fallen, or angel, or whatever they were. The pull to the house, and yet the urge to stay away nagged at the back of my mind. "Shut up, Damon." I suddenly didn't care if he hit me again.

His eyes narrowed, and a vein on his neck bulged. He dropped my chair back to four on the floor. He grinned and straightened. "You're in the middle of a war you know nothing about, and you don't have a friggin' clue how much you're involved." He grabbed the plates and headed into the kitchen, only to return with another full plate.

I felt tied to the chair, even when there were no ropes around me. "You're wrong. I'm not who you say I am." I ripped my collar down. "I've got no mark to prove it."

He paused, mouth full, and peered at my neck and partially exposed chest. "Maybe it's different for you. Maybe it shows up when you turn eighteen. When's your birthday by the way?" He shrugged and continued not giving me time to answer. "Seems you're the last of Bentos' offspring. Everyone else has been killed off." A fork full of chicken meat pointed in my direction. "Someone hid you well by sending you into foster care. It took us till last week to find out anything about you. When I told my Alpha what you'd said, I knew right away it was big. But you not having a clue...now that's priceless." He chuckled, shaking his head.

"I'm not a Grollic," I whispered. "I'm nothing."

"Yeah, by tomorrow you will be. Nothing, that is." With his thumb, he drew a line across his neck. "Shame really. You know nothing of who you are or what potential you could have. No one to inform or teach you – I wish I could say my heart bleeds, but it doesn't. I'm looking forward to tomorrow."

A long roar, followed by two short shouts echoed outside the cabin. A moment later, the sound repeated. Damon went to the window and stared out.

I blinked, surprised at how dark it was outside. Blacker than black.

Damon tapped the glass and pointed at several different locations. "There are twelve Grollics outside hoping you try to escape. I suggest, for the sake of your new family, you stay here. It'll give them a few more hours of living. Or maybe they care to meet up with the twelve Grollics at their cottage." He took his plate and as he headed to the kitchen, he added, "Sleep, sit, cry. Do whatever you want in here. The Grollics outside are ordered to kill if you go outside, and they will. If I were you, I wouldn't test them to find out."

I watched him walk out of the room and then turned my head toward the bay window. The only thing I could see was the room's reflection. How could I warn Michael and Grace to stay away? What weapon did I have on my side? Two measly bottles of liquor hadn't done jack. If I tried attacking Damon, he could handle me with one arm tied behind his back. My other option of sneaking out didn't look beneficial. Big hairy beasts lurking in the bushes outside ready to kill me on sight held little chance of survival.

I didn't stand a chance.

Damon said I knew nothing about who I was. Was there strength in that? I hit my palm against my forehead in frustration. I had a useless Grollic book I couldn't read.

I leapt from the chair, needing to pace to get my mind to think properly. *The Grollic book. That they know nothing about.* I moved, my palms gathering sweat. I might not be able to read it all, but I could read some. No one else could read it. If Bentos actually was my father –grandfather/whatever – could I read it because the book belonged to him? Could this book have found me because of who I was...because of my bloodline?

A warm feeling rose in my chest – a twinge of hope. Maybe there was a chance, a small possibility.

The momentary optimism disappeared when Damon returned from the kitchen, his eyes narrowing when he caught me pacing and saw the look on my face. My heart flip-flopped when his face darkened, his eyes turning an ugly yellow colour. He stomped over and shoved me hard onto the couch. Pain shot across my shoulders and up my neck when he grabbed my already bruised throat with both hands.

Chapter 14

"Don't try to figure some lousy plan. There's no way it'll work." With each word, he squeezed his fingers on my throat to match the cadence. Damon pulled his hand away, as if I burned him. "You pace, and you're going to bring the Grollics inside. Pacing makes them nervous," he said, getting inches away from my face, his hot breath blasting across my cheeks, "and we don't like anxiety. I want full glory for this, and if I have to kill you myself to bring you to my Alpha, I'll do it in a heartbeat. Don't piss me off!" He pushed away from me and swore under his breath.

Gasping for air, and unsure if my neck could handle another round of crush-testing, I clawed at my shirt trying to stretch the collar in an attempt to open my throat.

He dumped his large frame onto the other side of the couch, and banged his feet on the coffee table. He crossed his arms over his chest and scowled. "Don't screw this up. I might be the only one able to save you."

Horse shit. Blackmailing and kidnapping did not represent protection. He was using me. He wanted me dead. I refused to acknowledge him.

"Your friends are toast. I can't do anything for their kind. And you," he said, shaking his head, "deserve what's coming because you chose to associate with them."

Hands clenched, I stiffened and my eyebrows crushed together as I stared Damon down. His hair clung to his head, plastering itself to the sweat on the forehead of his contorted face. I'd never really hated anyone, but at this very moment, I hated Damon. I hated his Alpha leader, and the twelve Grollics outside the cabin. All of them, they didn't deserve to live.

I wished I had the Grollic book here. If Damon was telling the truth and if I was right about the book belonging to Bentos, everything would be seen in a different light.

I straightened and gasped: the book had been written to stop the Grollics, not understand them.

Glancing up, I turned to Damon. His head had fallen back, eyes closed and his chest rose and fell in a steady rhythm. Only a brainless Grollic like Damon could fall asleep at a time like this. *Maybe there's a weapon hidden somewhere in the cabin.* Quiet and with as least movement as possible, I slid from where I sat and snuck toward the hall.

A howl broke through the quiet night air. Damon jumped instantly alert. I moved to the couch in an attempt to drop into it and make myself disappear. The hair on the back of my neck prickled against my sweatshirt.

Damon walked to the front door and stuck his head out. Could he hear as well in human-form as when he's a Grollic?

Nothing. Only silence.

Then a short howl, further away, echoed in the night. Damon shut the door. He stretched and walked back over to the chair I'd previously occupied. "Nobody's coming to save you tonight. Your friends are searching the other side of town. They're not even close to the lake." He closed his eyes.

"You think I'm going to let you sleep?" It irritated me to think he'd just sleep. I'd probably be dead tomorrow and he had no issues of guilt or second thoughts. Had he killed before? "I have questions I deserve answers to."

He didn't bother to open his eyes, not even a tiny slit. "No."

"You're an ass. This is going to come back on you one day."

Damon heaved a huge sigh and sat up, rubbing his face. Without a word, he went into the kitchen and rummaged through the cupboards. Glasses clinked and then the tap water began running. He came back and handed me the glass. Before sitting back down, he set two white tablets on the coffee table. "Aspirin. Take them or I will. You're giving me a headache." He glared at me while I held the glass. His eyes turned dark when I refused to move. "At least drink the water, you're voice sounds like shit."

"That's 'cause you've been strangling me. I –"

"Drink it. Or I'll force it down your throat."

Not liking the amber color in his eyes, I brought the glass to my lips and swallowed down the lukewarm water. It tasted slightly metallic, coppery. I drank half, frowned and set the glass on the table, licking the roof of my mouth. "I'm not taking your little pills. Bull-crap they are aspirin."

Dick-head smirked and interlaced his fingers on his chest. "Fine. Now you'll sleep."

"No, I won't. I'm not..." I paused, wondering why my arms and head seemed suddenly heavy. Even my eyelids felt like they weighed fifty pounds each. Too late, I realized he'd used the aspirin as a ploy and drugged the water knowing I wouldn't take the pills. My upper body fell against the cushions behind me. Just before my head followed, and my mind sank into oblivion I mumbled, "You bas'sard."

A sharp pain along the side of my neck made me grimace behind closed eyes. I tried rolling my neck to stretch out the stiff muscle. When I inhaled a whiff of musty wet hair instead of the flowery scent of the pool house, I jerked and nearly fell off the couch.

I rubbed my neck where it had kinked. The groaned at the pain caused from the bruises that now probably covered my throat. Damon lay sprawled on the floor between the coach and the window. *Idiot's comatose and snoring.* He'd shoved the coffee table against the wall while I'd been out. The room misted with morning light.

Whatever Damon had snuck into the water had made me dead to the world, but didn't leave me feeling groggy. Either that or the thought of my eminent death cleared any residual effects away. I quietly stood and tentatively stepped over him to look out the window. It'd snowed more during the night.

Just as I lifted up my right leg to the other side of him, Damon grabbed my left ankle and sent me flying forwards. I turned, only to end up falling on my back and knocking the wind out of me. Damon pushed my feet, sending me sprawling across the wooden floor until the wall stopped my momentum. My head slammed against the wall and an instant headache spread. I was too stunned to move.

He crouched in an attack position, squatting on the balls of his feet. The noise that came out of his throat reminded me of the growl he had let out yesterday before turning into a Grollic. I stayed glued to the wall, terrified, but unable to look away.

The room became dead quiet, except for his mucus breathing. Still crouched, he shuddered and flexed his arms close against his body. "What the –?" His gaze narrowed in on me. He leapt to where I lay and with both hands, squeezed my shoulders painfully tight. He lifted me so his head and mine were level.

I tried to focus, his eyes swimming in circles from my head-butt with the wall.

"What the hell did you do?" he screamed and shook me.

Terrified, I tried to clear my thoughts and concentrate.

Obviously not fast enough from him, he held me by one arm and he slapped my face hard. "I'll ask you once more. This time, answer me or I break your arm."

I swallowed back the blood in my mouth oozing from my split lip. The side of my face burned and I ran my tongue over the swelling already forming on my lower lip. I blinked and tried to focus, scared he'd hit me again if I didn't answer fast enough. "I-I d-didn't do a-anything. I ha-haven't touched you."

"Lying spawn of Bentos! Whatever you did, FIX IT RIGHT NOW!!!" His face contorted as his lips curled over his teeth and his eyes shot daggers at me. The white and his pupils didn't change color. No burnt yellow, only bloodshot red.

"I don't know what you're talking about!" He'd bloomin' drugged me, not the other way around. Wait a minute. *The rye.*

"Bitch! I can't shift! Take back whatever you said and fix this." He grabbed my wrist and turned it painfully in the wrong direction. "I'll break every bone in your body until you do!"

Despite the situation, I croaked out a laugh. "It's not some voodoo curse, idiot. I didn't say something, and then add a no-take-backs."

Damon dropped his hold on me, and as I fell, he punched me in the gut. It stopped all laughter as I rolled on the floor and tried to catch my breath and stop the pain.

"The next contact will be my foot in your face!" The malice in his voice made me believe him. "What did you do?"

"I... Y-Yesterday, I... It was the ..." I struggled to find my breath. *Stomach muscles PLEASE relax. I beg you so I can inhale the oxygen I need.* I tried again, "Yesterday I made a drink to help me relax. You... You drank it."

"So what?" He brought his leg back.

"It was whiskey, you know... rye." I had no idea if he knew what that meant.

"You FED me RYE?" The spit from his shouting landed on my face.

I gagged. "You took my glass. You drank it." I rubbed the wet off my face terrified he'd ask me how I knew about rye.

"I'm going to kill you. Slow and painfully and before you die, I'm going show Michael. Watch the light die in his eyes when he sees you, and then kill him in front of you." He grabbed fistfuls of his hair. "I'm a Grollic who'll never shift again. That's more lethal than killing me!" He raised his leg again, ready to swing.

I scooted back against the wall, my hands up in defence. "I read... heard..." I couldn't make a lie up fast enough, "On the internet... that rye might possibly prevent a Grollic from changing. It's not forever. Just till the alcohol's out of your system. I had no idea it would work, and I never meant for you to drink it!" I tried to play the scared human victim. "I'm sorry! I didn't know this would happen."

He paused, setting his foot back on the floor. "It's not permanent?"

"Not that I know." *How long did I have?*

A long, horrible scream, followed by a short bark erupted from outside. My gaze shifted towards the windows, but I couldn't see anything from where I sat.

"Get your boots on." He grinned wickedly. "My Alpha approaches. It's time to go."

When I didn't move, he grabbed a handful of my sweater and tossed me onto the couch like a sack of potatoes. My heart thundered against my rib cage, or maybe it was my insides shaking that echoed against the beats. I slowly laced up my boots. With a sense of sadness I realized I could do nothing to stop the critical events about to maybe change, but more likely destroy my life.

Chapter 15

Damon had to physically pull me outside the door of the cabin. I no longer had the brain power to tell my body to put one foot in front of the other to walk. Cold air hit my face. It helped wake me a bit, however, I'd become numb inside. I could understand how a prisoner on death row felt on his last walk to the chamber. I shook my head to try to physically clear the fog out of my brain. I needed to focus and try to come up with something, anything. I had to fight.

Michael. His name made tears spring instantly to my eyes. I barely got to say good-bye to him yesterday. He had no idea how much I loved him or what he had done to bring color back into my life. I had spent the past eighteen years in shades of grey and black.

I had to wipe my tears with my shoulder when Damon grabbed my wrists and tied them together in front of me, with a rope trailing from them. I looked up confused. "Why? You never bothered binding me in the cabin?"

"I'm *not* having one of my so-called brothers claim my prize." He started walking through the trees, giving the leash I was now tied to a hard tug now and again. *Like a slave to his master.*

Tears continued to course down my face, as I trailed behind him. I couldn't stop Damon or figure out a way to live. Crying just helped feed the hopelessness.

I cried for everything I was going to miss out on with Michael. There was so much I wanted to know about him I would never get to learn. I would never get to share my life or experience anything with him. I should have told him how it felt to be with him. How we could talk, not just speak to each other. We connected as if we belonged together, like the Siorghra's eternal love.

Damon yanked the rope, forcing me to keep up. I stumbled, almost falling, when a new wave of sadness hit me. *Grace.* I bit into my lip to try and stop the tears, which didn't help because it broke open the cut Damon had given me earlier. I spat the iron taste out, the color bright crimson in the snow.

"Rouge!" Damon slapped my face hard enough to spin me around. I would have fallen if he hadn't tugged the rope which forced me to stay upright. Pain shot from my nose and up into my eyes. More blood dripped, this time from my nose. I tentatively touched it with my bound hands, scared it might be broken. Thank goodness it wasn't.

"Either start walking or I'll break your legs and actually have a reason to drag you." Damon's eyes darkened to a murky brown color.

I straightened, realizing the alcohol might be wearing off and he could change into a Grollic if he wanted to. I grew cold with fear and began to shake. Somehow, deep inside, I wasn't prepared for him to shift, like an inner sense wanted me to wait for the right moment. *Whatever that means... maybe after I die.*

I carefully nodded. "Sorry. I'll walk now." I knew enough from past life experiences that simple apologies and weak commitment might be adequate to avoid more violence. Pretending to feel bad and submit probably saved my legs from being broken. He turned and started walking again. I made sure to concentrate on following him.

As we walked through the almost knee-high snow, I tried to wipe my nose with the shoulder part of my sweater. The drops of fallen blood in the snow looked crimson compared to the brilliant white. My lip seemed to have stopped bleeding, and the blood from my nose slowed its rapid flow as well. I couldn't pinch it with my hands tied, so I tried pinching it with the inside of my elbow.

The sky was still a dull grey color, but in a few lighter shades. An eerie quiet filled the leaf-less forest. I could hear the odd twig break to the left or right of us every once in a while, but saw no one. When a loud crack echoed to my left, a huge, ugly grey Grollic appeared. Its hideousness made me shutter. Out of the corner of my eye, I caught sight of another to my right. They were probably flanked all around us to prevent Michael or anyone else from trying to rescue me.

We continued to hike around the lake but stayed inside the forest line. I wondered if walking by the frozen lake would leave the Grollics vulnerable to Michael's family. A strange thought crossed my mind. *Is there something about water Grollics don't like?*

Damon stopped when a very low and long howl erupted ahead of us – like a trumpet sounding. Damon pressed one knee to the ground, his head bowed and then stood. "My Alpha's approaching in Grollic-form." He shook himself and straightened his crumpled clothes. "If you care to live with hope of saving yourself or the Knightlys, don't you dare look him in the eyes. He'll kill you without a moment's hesitation." He leaned forward and freed my wrists from the tied rope digging into them.

More Grollics ret out the same howl as the first. We stood by a large tree. I leaned back against it for support, too tired to care if Damon bitched. Suddenly he dropped to one knee again and this time he didn't get up, or look up. My heart rate quickened as anxiety flowed through my veins. Searching every direction, I tried to spot what might be coming. The air grew heavy, like just before a thunderstorm. My breath caught in my throat from movement in the snow straight ahead.

At first I could barely make anything out, but as the trees became thicker the white fur became prominent against the bark. Moving at a speed which seemed impossible for any man or animal, the silhouette matched Damon's when he'd shifted.

Running towards us strode a terrifying, yet awesome creature. He was bigger than Damon, actually he made Damon look like a runt. The snow didn't shine nearly as much as the beast's coat and his eyes were a ruby red color. About twenty feet from us he slowed and rose to his hind legs... then walked like a normal human being, but still a Grollic. The beast had to be seven or eight feet tall. I jumped when he let out a guttural bark and stopped inches from Damon.

Damon rose slowly and leaned away from me. The Alpha ignored him and walked straight to me. His eyes narrowed and focused in on me. I tried to avoid meeting his gaze, as Damon had instructed, but I couldn't. The Grollic cocked his head to one side and stood inches away. He stared down, his hot, putrid breath slapping my face.

He had to weigh three hundred pounds, maybe more. He was massive, with not a speck of dirt on his white fur.

Craning my neck, I couldn't turn away even if I tried. The bright red of his eyes reminded me of blood, and I saw my reflection in them.

The beast made a noisy, wet sound as he inhaled. I cringed when his cold nose pressed against my neck and paused to smell the blood on my coat. I pressed myself closer into the tree trunk without even realizing until the rough bark scraped my cheek.

The Grollic stepped back and moved around the ancient tree. A second later he appeared on the other side in human form, completely naked. He must've been about fifty, extremely fit, white hair and the same birthmark as Damon just below his clavicle on the left side. His mark appeared darker and raised, almost as if burned onto his skin.

"This the one?" He looked at Damon.

I now had no problem avoiding my gaze. *He's apparently oblivious to the cold and snow.*

"Yes." Damon's head bobbed up and down.

"All this trouble for *her*?" He snorted and threw his hands up in the air. "It's weak and female! You're positive she's the seventh?"

"Seventh generation. Seventh descendent. Seventh of Bentos." Damon bounced up and down with each syllable. I wished I could wipe the grin off his face.

"Does the demon's offspring know?"

No, they've got no clue.

Damon scratched his birthmark. "She had no clue. If they know, they kept it from her."

They don't. Michael would've told me. Then why was I wondering if it might be true?

"Scoundrel," he scoffed. "Will they fight for her?"

"The twins will without a doubt. We're not so positive about Caleb. He's not too keen on the girl."

The Alpha leaned forward and slapped Damon across the face. Hard. Really hard. Howls erupted and glancing around, I nearly jumped up the tree to climb it. My heart exploded into rapid beating. The other Grollics had formed a semicircle around us. I hadn't noticed their approach. I'd been too focused on the Alpha. They were not as huge as the Alpha but big like Damon, and all different shades of ugly.

"Insolent!" the Alpha shouted at Damon. "I will not fight unless their Alpha is here! Why send for me if you're not sure?"

Damon cleared his throat. "We – I believe – Caleb will protect his understudy."

"And this girl, she is the offspring of Bentos? Without a doubt?" He asked the question again to Damon. Would a Grollic lie to his Alpha? How tight were their bonds?

Even in naked human form, the Alpha was terrifying. He charged toward my still frozen frame near the tree and grabbed my chin. Forcing my head left then right, he dropped his hand in disgust. "She stinks. Like liquorice. Her bloods tainted." He spat. As he spun around he swung back and pulled my collar down, scratching my skin. "She's not marked."

"She's the one." Damon shook and then whispered, "She is the last one, my lord."

The last? Of what? Had Damon somehow found me as the perfect target for this horrifying tirade and planned to use me to try and impress his Alpha?

"I'd don't believe it. She's a coward." He shook his head once. "Bait her for the Fallen, and kill her."

"With pleasure, my lord."

Suddenly a shaggy-haired Grollic came running out of the forest and jumped over the circle of Grollics. As it leapt into the air, it changed into human-form and dropped one knee down as he landed.

"What say you, scout?" the Alpha barked.

"Th-Three of th-them..." the young man panted. "One's fighting Janice at their cabin... Two are headed this way."

"The twins?"

"Two men, my lord. I believe one is their Alpha."

My heart skipped. *Michael and Caleb.*

The Alpha clapped his hands and rubbed them together. "Finally. I want that ol' bastard destroyed." He shot a glance at me. "Damon, take the girl by the water. Make sure they see her, and then drown her." He turned to the others, "You take the lesser male. *No one* kills the Alpha but me." He released a low hum which turned into a howl as he shifted into his grotesque Grollic-form.

Damon grabbed me, and threw me over his shoulder. He began to run towards the lake at breakneck speed. I bounced around and tried to keep my teeth clamped tight so I wouldn't bite my tongue.

"Put me down." I pounded against his back and tried thrashing my legs. He tightened his hold, his shoulder knocking the breath out of me as he dug it into my gut. My nose started to bleed again, and as I tried to suck air in through my mouth, I watched drops trail from my nose into the snow. I had nothing compared to the strength of Damon - human or shifted.

Tears sprang at the thought of Michael and the risk he was taking. I didn't want to die, but it seemed inevitable now. *Would Michael?* What could he do once surrounded by the pack of Grollics?

I continued the feeble beating of my fists on his back which probably acted more of an annoyance than causing any pain. I wanted to get back to dense forest and help Michael. *Do something, not be so weak and useless.* I hated myself, and despised the grollics even more.

Damon's running slowed to a walk and his arms came around my hips to toss me over him. I landed in a snowdrift and, angry as I felt, began shaking. I hadn't even realized the cold until the snow pressed against my bare skin and thin top.

Instinct made me stand and try to shake the snow off my exposed hands and wrists. I began rubbing my hands and blowing hot breath on them to warm them up. Blood mixed in with the snow and turned it crimson. Disgusted, I tried flicking it off.

Damon, standing fifteen feet away from me, laughed at my meagre attempt to create heat. The laughter stopped when I met his gaze. "What do think of your wonderful life now?" he mocked. "You're about to die, about to have your *immortal* boyfriend die, and all for what?

Nothing but a silent war I knew nothing about and an idiot saying I was the one they wanted dead.

"How ironic does it feel?"

I refused to answer. Ferocious growls and sounds fighting erupted in the forest, but here by the frozen lake, it was silent. With my back towards the water, I could feel the wind coming off it, making me shiver even more.

"You still don't get it, do you? Wait." He paused, tilting his head slightly. A grin full of scorn spread across his face. "You think you're one of them! You think, because you don't know your folks you might have *their* blood inside you." He snorted. "Impossible! You are the Seventh Mark."

My heart dropped lower than my stomach, which had just dropped itself. "I'm not marked," I whispered.

"Not above your chest." He pointed, his finger stabbing in my direction. "But you are. When you're dead, I'll cut your heart from your chest and find it. How about I show it to your boyfriend?"

My voice caught in my throat. I had nothing to say and nothing to protect Michael with.

"Answer me!" He snarled, and stepped closer, his arm now drawn back and hand balled tightly into a fist. "I want to see your fear and terror! How does it feel to know you are about to die from the one thing you despise? And I'm not going to kill you quickly. I promise you will hear Michael scream before I finish you off." He laughed a horribly, vicious laugh.

I forced my shoulders back and straightened, pissed at my own weakness and his pure evilness. "Screw you! You'll never be half the person Michael is. What do you have in your life? A pack of beasts who'll try to beat you any chance they get?" Damon's jaw tightened and his hands clenched together. *Ahhh, hit a nerve there.* It fuelled me with more courage. "An Alpha who doesn't give a toss if you live or die? You're expendable to him, you know? I'd choose torture and death over your life any day." I couldn't be sure if I now shook from rage or cold. "And here's something you don't know: I have Bentos' book. I know *everything*." I knew jack squat, but wasn't about to let him know that. I spread my arm out towards the forest. "I can kill you, and your whole damn pack."

Damon's face turned dark red. He growled, and his eyes burned dark, ugly yellow. Like the sun covered in blood. He took two steps and leapt, midair changing into Grollic.

Chapter 16

I stepped back and nearly fell rear-end into the snowdrift. Pushing my foot down hard through the snow, I managed to catch myself, for a second, before stumbling when the drift ended and I fell. Right onto the frozen lake. Facing the bank, I struggled to my knees and then tentatively stood, having to fight to keep my balance on the smooth ice.

Damon landed a few feet in front of me still on the ground. He snarled and swiped my arm with a paw. The claws caught me on my shoulder and ripped through my jacket and sweater. The sharp pain came instantly and I fell, sliding further onto the frozen lake. Damon sat on his hunches not venturing off the snow. He tried to swipe again but I leaned out of reach. Wind from the swing shot by my face making me flinch. He snarled, flashing sharp, yellow teeth.

"What's the matter? You scared of ice?" I jeered as I rose, struggling again to keep my balance. The ice was smooth like a mirror. "What'll your precious Alpha think of you when he hears this?" *Silly girl taunting a Grollic.* He probably couldn't even understand in beast form.

He growled. Leaning forward, he tried to take another hit at me again. I shuffled back. Better safe than dead. The monster paced the edge of the lake. Would he turn back into a human and step onto the ice to kill me?

The matted, greasy hair on his back rose and he glanced back toward the forest as a vicious howl erupted and suddenly cut off. I hoped he'd run back to the fighting. No luck. A small cry shot out of my throat when he turned and pushed off the bank onto the ice toward me.

Eyes wide, I struggled to keep my legs from slipping as they tried to move backwards as fast as they could. The beast leaped into the air with his jaw open, aiming for my throat. *Or anywhere in that vicinity... probably my heart.*

Instinct made me cringe, and my feet slid out from under me. My head hit hard against the frozen water, but an ear curdling growl told me Damon had missed me and hit the ice instead.

I rolled to watch him struggle on the ice. His four paws slipped out from underneath his massive weight. A resounding crack of the ice echoed loud in the air and he thumped underneath me.

Crawling on my hands and knees, I edged towards the bank and lurched myself on the snow the moment I hit it. I swore Damon's breath was brushing against my neck. I pushed upright and began running hard, needing as much of a head start on land as I could get. Just over the snow drift, a loud cracking noise sounded again, followed by a terrified yelp.

I glanced behind and froze in my tracks.

The ice gave way and Damon disappeared into the cracked ice.

Water splashed as he struggled to get a clawed grip onto the frozen wet ice around him. Just as he seemed to be gaining ground, his paw slipped and Damon disappeared from the small opening. Muffled thumps echoed under the ice as he struggled to break through from beneath its surface. The noise slowed, weakened and eventually stopped.

My heart beating so fast I was sure it would explode, I scanned the lake and waited for the monster to break through. My head tried to tell me what my eyes and body would not believe. *Nothing's coming out of the ice.*

He died instead of me.

At least, I wasn't going to die at that exact moment or place. Now I had a chance to help Michael.

His name brought me out of my frozen state. I turned and raced back into the forest, terrified I'd now be too late. My shoulder blade burned. I pumped my arms to move faster. The pain only made me push harder.

As I got closer the noise became deafening. Each contact of body with tree and each growl reverberated against my chest.

I slowed my pace to assess the situation and possibly sneak in without being noticed. I stepped over a dead Grollic, blood oozing from a jagged cut in its neck, and hid behind a tree to locate Michael and Caleb.

Back against the tree, I closed my eyes and took a few deeps breaths. Part of me still thought Damon would burst through the trees. Deep down, I knew he was dead, but fight or flight continued to wreak havoc with my brain process. Peering from the one side of the bark, my heart rate quickened with what I saw.

Michael.

Covered in blood, he still looked very much alive as he fought against two massive beasts. His fighting seemed like a dance he led with the Grollics trying to keep up.

Caleb and Seth's lack of appearance set my teeth to chatter. I squinted to focus on Michael, and as if I had mentally called to him, his head turned slightly toward me. His eyes widened and immediately his fight took on a stronger vengeance. Leaping off the ground, his feet connected with one Grollic's chest and he used that momentum to get higher into the air, one arm bent back. He moved so fast, I only caught the glimmer of silver before it sunk deep into the other Grollic's chest. Before the beast hit the ground, Michael pulled the blade out and stabbed it again and again. He repeated another four times in the same area and then wiped the blade on his pant leg.

Mesmerized, I could only watch. There were still seven Grollics attacking, but he continued to fend them off. It dawned on me that they were working on surrounding him, trying to encircle and tire him. They began attacking him two at a time, then pulled back to have two others attack before quickly retreating for another two Grollics. *A game. A bloody, taunting game.* I swore I heard their laughter.

Michael began to slow from fending off mortal bites and gouging claws. The Grollics fighting skills seemed meticulous. There were a lot of them, but they fought as if they were one mind.

Horrified, I could only cover my mouth to keep back the scream when Michael sustained a huge swipe from a pair of claws down his back. It looked like he had been whipped five times.

He stumbled from the blow, his eyes closed and nostrils flaring. He pressed his lips tight as if refusing to show anything.

He needed help, and I was the only one here. Who knew where Caleb could be. *Or if he's still alive?*

A howl erupted as two Grollics managed to pin Michael down. Michael kicked and thrashed in the snow, the white turning to crimson and brown. He managed to free one arm, and clasped it under him only to pull it out a mere second later with a long, thin blade. Faster than my brain could register, he sunk the dagger into the Grollic holding him down. The beast fell, flaying as he went and going limp seconds later.

Before Michael had a chance to react, another Grollic grabbed both Michael's arms and pinned them high above his head. The Grollic gnashed his teeth and barked at another Grollic nearby. It came toward Michael, his mouth opened wide. Straight for Michael's neck!

I couldn't stay hidden and watch him die. I jumped out from behind the tree and in clear view of the Grollics, I whistled. The hands in your mouth, screaming whistle. The terror in Michael's eyes scared even me. He shouted "NO!" and struggled harder against the Grollic holding him down.

Another monster turned and reared, already pushing towards me into a jump of attack. His jaws were open the way Damon had just come after me. Without even consciously thinking, I shouted, "*Vilkacis Diakonos!*" The words came from the Grollic book.

Wild static hit the air followed by a silent, almost sonic, boom. The one Grollic stopped mid-flight and dropped into a lying position at my feet. The others instantly stopped their attack on Michael and dropped onto their haunches, each staring directly at me.

The area became dead quiet. The Grollics did not move, as if waiting for something... someone. *Their Alpha?*

Michael still lay on the ground, his chest heaving.

"Are you hurt?" I asked, unsure that if I moved, the Grollics would break from their strange, almost frozen state.

It seemed like eons before he pushed himself up and stood slowly. His eyes never left my face. I think the expression on my face must have been similar to his dumbfounded one.

"What did you do?" he whispered.

I hesitated, afraid to look away from his face. "I-I-I'm not exactly sure." I tore my gaze from his ice blue eyes to the mammoth Grollics now sitting like good little puppies. My eyes narrowed as I recalled how intent they'd been on killing me and Michael. They were following orders from their Alpha, but I could feel their hatred towards us even as they sat, unable to move.

Waiting. *Waiting for orders from me.* I knew it without doubt. The answer ran through my veins...In my blood.

"Go! All of you! Head to the lake" I pointed at each one. "Every one of you—"

Caleb appeared from behind a large tree, Seth close on his heels. Both had signs of fighting, but were alive. They dropped into a crouch position, Seth pulling a long blade from behind the side of his boot.

The Grollics growled but none made a move or even slightly rose from their sitting positions. Their eyes darted towards Seth and Caleb, but constantly came back to focus on me.

Caleb started to speak and Seth seemed about to pounce. I panicked and cleared my throat loudly. I needed to finish whatever I'd planned on saying before I lost control of the pack and somebody got himself killed. Blinking, I tried to focus, not sure what to do. *What if the Alpha came back?* Glancing at the spray of blood across Caleb's coat, I assumed it wouldn't be. "Head to the lake, all of you, and find where the ice is thinnest." I swallowed. "Join Damon under the ice. Your Alpha is defeated and dead. If you manage to survive, change back to human form and forget all of this. Forget you were ever a Grollic, that you ever saw me, or any of us. Live your life with no memory of being a beast." I glanced at Caleb who stared at me with blue eyes large as golf balls. His mouth hung open, but he said nothing. Even Seth's face had shock written all over it.

I snapped my fingers and pointed in the direction of the lake. "Go! Now." The Grollics tore past me toward the lake. There was no sound but their paws hitting the snow followed by the slap of water as they jumped into the hole where Damon had disappeared into. Each splash made me cringe and I grew colder and colder.

Michael rushed to me and caught me just as my knees gave way. He pulled me into his arms and didn't say anything, only held me tight against him.

"What the hell just happened?" Caleb hollered.

"Not now." Michael's voice came out crisp and clear. "Rouge needs warmth or she's going to die from hypothermia." Without another word, he picked me up and started walking. Seth and Caleb followed alongside.

Exhausted, I let my head fall against the warmth of Michael's muscular chest. Before dropping my lids, I caught sight of Seth's grin as he winked at me.

The steady bouncing of my head and body from the rhythm of Michael's walk made my body relax. *Michael's safe, alive and holding me.* I slipped deeper into him.

I jolted awake when Michael's walk changed and his thighs brushed again my back. We were going up steps. Caleb's cabin. The sun had begun to drop but the broken glass and splintered door were impossible to miss. The cabin had taken a beating, from the inside out.

Michael gracefully stepped over the splintered wood and headed straight for the torn, but still in one piece, couch. "Seth, get the fire going. Caleb, is there any food here?"

"Of course. Why wouldn –"

"Go get something. And warm it up."

Caleb scowled at Michael and crossed his arms over his massive chest. He stood, staring down at me, not going to the kitchen.

Exhausted, and my shoulder burning, I didn't have the strength to fight him. "Caleb, what d'you want?" *Screw politeness.*

"It appears you are a lot more useful than the typical human."

"Get the food!" Michael shouted, glaring at Caleb.

"Fine. I'll get it." He returned the glare. "But she needs to answer some questions."

"I'll get the wood." Seth stepped outside and bent down. He came back in carrying the remains of the door. He grinned and shrugged. "No sense in keeping this."

He kneeled down and got to work on the fire. Michael stayed close to my side, trying to check my shoulder. I kept swatting his hand away. We could look at the cut later. It stung but my arm wasn't going to fall off.

Caleb returned with a steaming cup. He handed it to me and tossed a bag of chocolate chip cookies on the couch.

I took a tentative sip. The tea was hot and tender on my cut lip, but deliciously warm going down. I blew lightly and then took a few longer sips and set the cup in my lap. "Are Grace and Sarah all right?"

"They're fine," Michael said. "They're on their way here with medical supplies."

"And a change of clothes?" I wasn't staying in these dirty Grollic-girl's clothes.

"Of course." Michael moved slightly, letting the warmth of Seth's fire reach me.

"Thank you." I lifted my tea and drank again.

"Enough of this ridiculous tender moment." Caleb's right foot began tapping against the floor, the broken glass crackling under the pressure.

Michael glared at him until Caleb stopped tapping. "Tell us what happened – from the beginning." Michael's voice became soothing, and he took my free hand and held it in both of his warm hands.

Where do I start? "Yesterday." It seemed crazy it was only yesterday. I could have sworn I'd been apart from Michael for a lot longer. "I-I took the Jeep to the grocery store to pick up stuff for dinner. I talked Grace out of coming along. She insisted so don't be mad at her—I honestly didn't think I was in any danger." Michael raised his eyebrows but said nothing. Caleb harrumphed.

I pulled my hand free from Michael and tucked a chunk of hair behind my ear. "Damon jumped into the passenger seat and told me the Grollics had captured Grace and Sarah. The only chance they had was if I went along with what he wanted. He told me to drive to your cabin and some girl met us. Damon made us exchange clothes."

Seth, now leaning an elbow on the fire mantel, interrupted, "That's why I could smell you in the cabin and outside. I didn't catch her scent until a moment before she tried to attack. Your licorice scent hid hers." He looked at me. "She's dead. Not in here, but dead."

I swallowed, slightly relieved not to have to see, but also curious if he'd killed her as beast or human. *Morbid idiot.*

Caleb purposely cleared his throat.

I shot him a look. "Then Damon hiked me through the forest to another cabin on the other side of the lake."

"I caught your scent and found the cabin," Michael said.

I shrugged, grimacing from the pain that shot from my shoulder. It lingered near my shoulder blade at the back. "How?"

"I found strands of your hair."

The hair I'd absently shaken from my hands. A trail I'd never meant to leave. "I had no idea what he, or they, planned. I didn't want any of you to die." I met each of their gazes. "He kept me imprisoned there until morning. The other Grollics surrounded the house to stop me from leaving or anyone from coming in."

"Why you?" Seth asked.

My mouth suddenly went dry. I took a small sip of tea and then whispered, "Damon said I'm related to *Bentos* – somehow I am his grandchild or something like that. I am so sorry." My eyes filled, waiting for Michael to jump away like I know I burned him.

Now he'd hate me, and Caleb would start cursing the day I was born. I let my head drop, the tears escaping my eyes and running down my cheeks.

Michael's fingers touched my chin and forced me to meet his gaze. His eyes were soft... sincere. "Are you okay?"

"You're not mad?" How could he be worried about me?

"Mad?" he sounded confused. "Why would I be mad? You think I care about who your father or grandfather or even your great-grandfather is? I fell in love with *you* for who *you* are, not your past. You love me unconditionally, how can you not expect the same in return?" He leaned over and kissed me on the cheek, avoiding my cut lip.

"Thanks," I whispered. "You keep giving me more reasons to love you." I reached out and touched his face with my fingertips.

Caleb swore under his breath. "What happened today?"

Did Caleb already know? "Damon dragged me into the forest to meet his Alpha." I rested my elbows on my knees. "Their Alpha wanted to use me as bait to get Michael, and he wanted to fight you. He wanted me dead, then Caleb. The rest of you would be a bonus." I shook my head. "I don't get why they want me dead. If I'm one of them... wouldn't they want me serving their Alpha? Damon said those who are marked can shift when they turn eighteen. He said I'm marked, but I'm not."

Caleb began pacing. "You are the one weapon they can do nothing to control or destroy. The Seventh Mark. I've never clearly understood its meaning." He stopped moving and stared directly at me. "They needed you dead before you realized the potential of your power."

He was ticked. I didn't get it. I wasn't marked. Whatever happened out there had been a fluke. I tried to explain again. "The Alpha seemed a lot older than the pack, and while they were all browns, blacks, and greys, he was pure white with spooky red eyes. He's—"

"Not very white now, more of a rust color," Seth joked.

"What happened?" I looked from Caleb to Seth, forgetting my train of thought.

"After I finished here with the girl, I raced off to find Michael and Caleb. Seems your white Grollic assumed I was Caleb and tried to attack. Imagine his surprise when I fought with him and then Caleb showed up." Seth grinned at Caleb sheepishly. "Sorry, but who could resist playing leader?" Seeing Caleb's face harden, he added, "I stepped down the minute you showed up."

"Yes, and rightly so, sheep," Caleb said. "The Alpha was more bark than bite."

I was confused. How could they tell who which beast was the better in the battle? They were all scary monsters and I definitely had no plans to meet any more. I shuddered, hating them, and now hating myself even more.

"What happened in the forest, Rouge?" Michael reached for my hand again.

"Damon dragged me down to the lake. Oh, I forgot to tell you I tricked him into drinking whiskey. I read in the book that rye could prevent a Grollic from shifting. It won't stop them forever, just until the alcohol has cleared their body. He got pretty mad at me in the cabin when he realized I had tricked him. Anyway, it didn't last long enough. Damon jumped to attack me at the lake, and I ducked. He flew over me and landed on the ice. He must have landed on a thin part...it cracked an-and h-he went under." The image burned like an old movie in my mind.

"What do you mean about *rye?*" Caleb demanded.

"It seemed silly at the time, but in the book it mentioned rye would act as an inhibitor. I wasn't sure if it had to be in natural form or if it didn't matter. I picked up two mini shot bottles of whiskey-rye at the grocery store and thought I might just keep them in my purse, you know, in case I might need them. It sounded really silly to me at the time, so I hadn't mentioned it to Michael, or any of you." I squeezed Michael's hand, and he returned the same pressure.

"Do Grollics know about this weakness?" Caleb continued to press me.

"Damon didn't seem to know. He was pretty ticked off when he tried to change and suddenly couldn't." I touched my face, feeling the puffiness and wondered how bad I looked. "He thought I'd done some voodoo thing, like I could say something and stop him from changing." I shrugged but didn't miss the exchanged look between Michael and Seth. "He definitely didn't know alcohol was a possibility. He didn't drink much, so I wasn't sure if it would work or for how long ... it was more of a guess on my part."

"An experiment," Seth corrected, smiling.

"A gut instinct," Michael added, a little more serious.

"Sure, whatever. I really didn't think it would work, but it was worth a shot as I figured I'd be dead by the end of the day."

Michael pulled me tight against him. He buried his face in my hair and inhaled deeply. He whispered in my ear, "No, very much alive."

"I was terrified Damon was going to bite me and turn me into a Grollic. I didn't know it's a blood-line thing. Nobody told me." I turned purposely to Caleb and began tapping my foot.

"Point noted, we'll tell you everything we know about Grollics next time." Caleb snorted. "If you don't already know it all. Now, would you please tell us what you did to the Grollics and why you bothered to not inform us of your ability?"

I straightened and blinked. "I don't know what I did." I couldn't keep the frustration out of my voice and directed it towards Caleb. "Don't you think I'd have told you if I knew? I'm living under your roof, in love with your understudy, best friends with his twin, and YOU THINK I WOULD KEEP THIS A SECRET?" I stood indignantly. I pushed Michael's reaching hands away and marched up to Caleb. Shame I was so short compared to him, I still had to look up to him.

He glared down at me but said nothing.

"Don't you think I'd have preferred to avoid this entire situation and would've turned those beasts into pulp if I knew I could? I got the crap beaten out of me – that is something any *human* would try to avoid!" I was yelling, now beyond rage. Everything that had built up over the past few days was being unleashed on Caleb, and I didn't care. "You, Mr. Higher Coven, have NO answer to what or who I am. You might think you know, but you haven't got a clue." I poked him in the chest, hurting my finger with the pressure. Caleb didn't even flinch. It pissed me off more. "I've spent my entire life as a nothing. Not knowing who my parents were, why no one wanted me, or what I'd done to fate to deserve all this misery. I meet Grace and Michael and, for the first time in my life, feel like I have a reason to live. And you want to tell me I planned this?"

"Rouge," Michael warned.

I ignored him. "I don't know how that stupid book ended up in my hands – maybe it was fate, maybe luck. I don't freakin' know! I don't ever want to open it or read it again. If I never see another Grollic again, it'll be too soon!! I'm glad they're all freakin' gone!" My chest heaved, but I refused to let my gaze leave Caleb's face.

"They are NOT gone," Caleb hissed back. "There are more and if this pack knew about you, rest assured, the others know as well." He scowled, his eyes burning bright blue. "Now, what the hell did you do at the lake to those monsters?"

My anger evaporated. "There're more?"

Caleb was right, they probably all knew about me or of the offspring of Bentos. Suddenly this nightmare felt like it was just the beginning.

"What happened, Rouge?" Michael's calm voice strengthened me.

I flopped down onto the couch beside him, grimacing as my aching body protested. "After Damon disappeared under the ice, I ran back to the noise." I turned to Seth. "Michael was fighting them all off, but there were so many. Then one saw me and came toward me. I didn't think. The words were out of my mouth before I realized."

"What words?" Seth curiously asked.

I had no idea if I'd even pronounced them correctly. They were written in the Grollic book, in the part I don't know how to read. Curling my toes, I knew trying to explain it wouldn't make sense. "They...They just popped into my head."

"What words?" Caleb pressed.

"*Vilkacis Diakonos.*" I glanced around and held my breath, expecting to feel the weird static and sonic boom again. Nothing happened.

"Do you know what it means?" Michael asked.

"I do now." I stuck my palm toward Caleb, stopping him from talking. "Don't ask me how. *Vilkacis* means Grollic-eyes. *Diakonos* means one who serves. It's what Bentos said that let him control those beasts." I exhaled slowly. "Michael saw what happened when I repeated them."

"I felt something. Like heavy static hit the air and zing through each of the Grollics." Michael turned to Seth and Caleb. "The Grollics stopped fighting and just dropped to a sitting position. Waiting...waiting for Rouge."

"That's when you and Seth came," I said, rubbing my temples. "I understood their hatred for you. I could sense all of their emotions and their frustration at me controlling them. They could do nothing."

"But when you spoke to them," Caleb said. "It wasn't English. You spoke in a different tongue."

What? I looked at him incredibly. *Impossible.* He had to be joking. I had spoken in English – plain and clear. "Excuse me?"

"You weren't speaking English." Caleb spoke as if I were slow.

"Yes, I was. I don't speak Grollic." My voice rose, but seeing Michael shake his head, I grew confused. "I don't know any other language."

"It's the language of the Grollic book. It's from Bentos. He created it." Caleb spoke to no one in particular, but sounded so sure. "What did you tell them, as we obviously couldn't translate what you said?" His tone was no longer condescending, only curious.

"They wanted to attack but couldn't...because of me. I felt their hatred for you and how much they wanted to kill Michael, and all of you. It made me mad, angry enough that I wanted them all dead. I told them to go into the water where Damon had drowned."

Seth started laughing.

All of us looked over at him.

It took a few moments, but he finally got control of himself. Still grinning, he said, "You're basically telling us that you told them to go jump in the lake – as the saying goes." He roared with laughter again.

"Funny, Seth, really funny!" I stood. "Maybe I should tell you to go jump in the lake!"

Michael started laughing at my snide remark. Seth stopped, his face serious and also a little paranoid. "Wait, can you control us as well?"

I grabbed my mug off the couch and drilled it at him. He ducked easily and the porcelain mug shattered against the wall behind him.

"Apparently your new talent has Caleb intrigued." Seth pointed over to Caleb who nodded his head.

"Great! Now I really am a freak!!"

"Nah, sweetie." Seth chuckled. "It just makes you a bit more like us and a little less human."

No one commented and the silence stretched out.

Suddenly, all I really wanted to do was go home. To the pool house, have a bath, and crawl into bed. Sleep sounded wonderful. The shock started to wear off and my body began to ache from the bruises and cuts.

Michael sensed my body's reaction and lifted me into his arms as he stood.

"Caleb, Rouge needs to get back. She's exhausted and her wounds must be tended to. You and Seth clean up any mess in the forest. The last thing we want is authorities looking into what happened. Burn the bodies of the dead Grollics and check the lake. Seth, double check for any tracks – human or Grollic."

He didn't wait for their reply. He simply walked out the door and carried me to the Jeep. He set me gingerly onto the passenger seat and buckled me in. He kissed my forehead before shutting the door and ran around to the driver's side. I couldn't keep my eyes open and let my head fall forward as Michael started the Jeep and pulled away from the cabin. I wanted to tell him that I had put his Siorghra under the driver's seat, but utter exhaustion crept in before I could even say a word.

Chapter 17

I must've passed out the entire ride back to the house... and then some. I don't know for how long, but when my brain became alert again it was from behind closed eyes and the comforting of my own bed underneath me. I heard the kettle steaming, moved against the firm mattress under me, and then... soreness everywhere. My head, my neck, my back and my shoulder. *Shoot, even the back of my eyelids hurt.* I groaned and buried deeper into the soft blanket, begging the pain to stop. Somehow I drifted into a restless sleep.

Cool air danced around me and with a floppy arm I lazily reached for the now missing duvet. I fought to open my crusty eyes when I realized Michael was carrying me. And I lay in his arms wearing only a tank top and underwear.

"Michael, I..." My breath escaped in a loud huff. Pain shot everywhere with each movement.

He lowered me into a bath full of wonderfully warm water. "Shh... Rouge. Just relax and soak in the hot. It's salt water. It'll help your muscles and clean your cuts. Grace is coming to help." He kissed my forehead and disappeared.

My eyes dropped shut again, too heavy and sore to keep open.

Moments later a gentle knock at the door and cool air against my damp skin let me know Grace had come. I sensed her kneel down beside the tub.

"You silly girl," she whispered. "Why didn't you let me go with you?" She didn't push for a reply. "I'll wash your shoulder. It's looking pretty nasty. When you're out of here we'll bandage it properly."

A soft cloth brushed against my arm as she dipped into the hot water. I gave a slight nod.

"This is going to hurt a bit," she said and paused. "Can you slide down a bit deeper and let the water clean the cut first?"

I arched my toes and let my bum slide against the bottom of the tub. A cry escaped my lips when the soothing water turned to burning acid on my shoulder. My eyes shot open. "Holy Shi—!"

Grace poured a cup of water over my head to stop the cascade of swearing escaping my lips.

I sputtered and spit the water out. The salt seeped into my cut lip and along my cheek, making everything sting. I glared at her.

"Sorry." She grinned. "You needed to get rid of the dried blood out of your nose, lips, and hair." She shrugged and pointed at my face. "If I were you, I'd avoid rubbing your lips or pressing them tight like you are right now. They'll take forever to heal and somebody's gonna wanna smooch those." She paused then added loudly, "Yeah, Michael. I'll shut up."

I smirked. Point for Michael. "I can wash myself."

"Fine. But you can't reach your back. Let me get the cut and dried blood cleaned on that side. Lean forward." She grinned. "Please."

I nodded, feeling better already and slid forward. "Wash away."

Grace wiped and dabbed. Her hand, even warm against the tub water, touched the edge of my shoulder blade, close to my spine and near the bottom. She rubbed the wash cloth over the spot a few times, pressing harder with each stroke. "The dried blood's not coming off." She leaned forward. "Oops, it's your birthmark. Weird. It's turned black. Didn't it used to be red, but now it's... Oh. My. Gosh." She gasped and jumped back, her eyes and mouth open wide.

Then she did the strangest thing, she sniffed the air.

What the heck?

"Still liquorice."

"What?" I tried to twist to see it, but everything hurt and I'd never been able to see it properly anyway since it lay in such an awkward spot. I reached awkwardly, trying to find the mark.

Blue eyes bigger than I'd ever seen on her, she blinked rapidly. "It looks like it's been burned." She straightened and dropped the wash cloth. "I-I think you can do the rest yourself."

I grabbed her wrist before she could escape. "What are you not telling me?" I spoke barely a whisper. My heart thundered against my chest. I gripped her tiny arm with a strength I never knew I had.

Michael banged on the door. "Is everything okay?"

I tugged Grace's arm. "We're fine," I called to Michael, and then mouthed to Grace, "What?"

She grazed her teeth over her bottom lip and then leaned forward, so close I could feel her lips press my ear as she spoke, barely above a whisper. "Yours is the same mark the Grollic has on their chest, by their heart. It's in the same spot, just on your back. By *your* heart."

The Seventh Mark. Damon's haunted words echoed inside my head. "It doesn't mean anything." The words were false but I said them anyway. I glanced at the door then back at her and shook my head.

"I won't." She knew I didn't want Michael to know—yet.

"I'm okay to finish on my own." I let go of her wrist and reached for the wash cloth.

"You sure?" Grace seemed relieved. "Let me grab you a towel and robe." She disappeared through the door and told Michael to make some tea. She came back a moment later and set the soft fluffy towel and robe on the counter. "Call me if you need help getting out." She grinned sheepishly. "Just so you know; the same still goes, 'kay? I like you for who you are, not the past." Then she was gone again.

I sank back down into the now cooling water.

Could Michael have heard our conversation? My heart thumped against my rib cage. Maybe he hadn't paid attention and figured it was girl stuff we were whispering about. Would she tell him? Or worse, tell Caleb? I rubbed my temples. Her instant change in reaction worried me. Needing a distraction, I washed and soaked until the kettle began to whistle. I slowly got out of the tub. Using scissors from a drawer I cut the tank shoulder straps and then carefully wrapped myself into the bathrobe. Ugly purple, green and blue blotches covered my body. The four jagged, welted lines on my shoulder looked angry so I left the robe to hang off my shoulder and let them air dry.

I like you for who you are, not your past. The meaning of Grace's words sunk in. She didn't care. She'd risk everything to be friends with the enemy, the forbidden.

In bare feet, I padded back to the main room, and slowly lowered myself to the futon bed. Soft and inviting. It eliminated my worries about Grace—for the moment.

Michael walked over carrying a tray and set it down on the bed beside me.

"It's safe, I didn't make it. Emily made the soup." He gave a quick smile. "I did make the tea and it's herbal, so I can't really screw it up." He pointed to a little bear. "Just in case, there's some honey."

The soup smelled good. My tummy rumbled in agreement. "How long have I been sleeping?"

"All night." Michael reached over and grabbed a brown paper bag from the chair beside the bed. "And most of the day."

I glanced out the windows. The grey clouds hid the sun so I couldn't tell if it was afternoon or dusk.

"Eat. I'll fix your shoulder."

My heart sped to an erratic rhythm again. "My shoulder?"

Gauze, tape and bandages were dumped out of the bag. "I promise it won't hurt." He lifted two fingers. "Scouts' honor."

Warmth crept to my cheeks and face.

Michael chuckled. "Feeling modest? Don't worry. I'll keep my eyes averted." He kissed me lightly on the lips.

Even his touch didn't distract me from my worry. *If he sees my birthmark. If he knows.* I held my breath. *If he heard what Grace said, he'll make sure to see it now.* I grimaced.

"Sorry." Michael quickly leaned back, obviously mistaking my facial expression for pain. "I know it hurts, but we need to get those wounds healed."

He moved around to bandage my entire shoulder and true to his word, kept his eyes on my face, only double checking the tape. If he knew about my birthmark, he never said. I'll tell him another day, when I'm a bit stronger. Or when I'm forced to tell.

I ate two bowls of soup and drank the tea (with a spoonful of honey). Michael cleared the dishes and then settled beside me.

"Do you think the claw marks will scar?" A constant reminder of Damon.

"I don't know. It doesn't matter, does it?" Michael said. "It's just a mark. Something to show where you've been and how you made it through."

"I like that." I rested my head on his chest. He smelled wonderful.

"Good." He sighed, taking my hand in his and tracing his thumb along the top of mine. "I was so worried about you, and when I saw you come charging towards me while fighting those Grollics, it terrified and thrilled me at the same time. I still don't fully understand what you did, but you're safe, and that's all that matters."

I smirked, then had to stop from the soreness. "I figured you needed some help." I tried to hide a yawn, but it snuck out. "You needed a knight in shiny armour and I happened to be around."

"Sleep. You need it. We can talk tomorrow."

I closed my eyes. An image of Damon's mark flashed behind my lids, this time on my back. "Don't leave me, please?" I whispered.

"I'm here all night –"

"I mean ever. Don't ever leave."

He squeezed my hand. "I'm not going anywhere. My place is by your side. Now sleep." He kissed the top of my head.

Early the next morning, I woke from trying to shift my legs. I hurt all over. If that was even possible. Every muscle and bone ached, even my skin screamed at me to lie still. I tried to hold in a groan, but it escaped. Michael instantly sat up with concern, which didn't help as his sudden movement caused me to drop from his shoulder to the bed.

I cried out and swore. It took a moment to catch my breath. "I'm a little sore," I whispered hoarsely.

Michael nodded, his eyes full of sympathy.

"I guess being thrown across the room and hitting a wall makes the average human a little tender," I joked. "I saw Caleb throw you and you got up like nothing happened."

"It did hurt, but by the time I stood, any broken bones were healed. I was pretty ticked off that night to even notice the pain."

"Maybe I've cracked a rib or two. I'm really aching." I tried to grin and make light of how I felt. "It could be a lot worse."

"Don't even go there." Michael shook his head. "Been one heck of a weekend, and it's only Sunday."

I groaned. "I've already missed a week of school." I'm officially eighteen. The thought made my shoulder burn.

Michael leaned over and grabbed his phone from the night stand and started to check his messages. "I wouldn't worry too much. Grace can go tomorrow and get the work you've missed." His eyes scanned his phone. "Caleb wants to see us." His fingers began tapping over the keys. "I'll text him to wait till tomorrow."

I lay quiet a minute, thinking about the past few days and what Damon had said. When Michael put his phone down I spoke my thoughts aloud. "I'd like to find out about my past. Damon said I'm the seventh descendent of Bentos. If the Grollics could find out about my history, so can I."

"I bet we can find something online," Michael said, lightly rubbing my arm. "And I can ask Caleb. He's got connections."

"This is something I want to do on my own. For the first time in my life, I'm curious to know who my parents are, or if they're still alive. I need to do this myself, and I need to go back to Niagara Falls." Childish hope still filtered through my thoughts. I wanted to know if my mother had tried to hide me, or if there was another reason why I knew nothing. I also needed to figure out the freaky birthmark on my back. "You know, I'd really like to know how I landed up with the Grollic book."

"Maybe it was destiny, and the book found you." Michael wrapped his long arms around his knees and clasped his hands together. "Fate has its own plans. I've learned that you don't mess with them."

He looked so cute, and young sitting like that. Too young to be spouting about destiny and fate. I forced myself to sit and brought my legs over the side of the futon bed. I groaned as I reached for my jeans.

"Rouge, take it easy. We're not leaving now."

"I know, but now I have some questions for Caleb."

Chapter 18

It took a bit of time getting dressed and trudging through the snow to the house, but I managed. If I closed my eyes and focused on breathing through the pain, maybe I could wish and force the soreness and bruises to heal faster. Even though Michael offered several times to carry me, I refused. I wanted" I needed to do this on my own.

Grace met us at the door, with a wrinkled brow and eyes full of worry as they flitted back and forth between us. 'Everything alright?"

'Fine," Michael said. 'We need to talk to Caleb."

'He-s-in his office with Seth." Grace continued to stand in the doorway. She must have realized she was blocking us out as she suddenly jumped back. 'Sorry."

Michael nodded and with his arm tucked tightly against my waist, he helped me to the office. He rapped on the wood once and pushed the door open.

'Rouge!" Seth stood leaned against a case of books but jumped and rushed toward us. He leaned in to hug me, but Michael put a strong hand on his chest and simply shook his head once.

Embarrassed, I stuttered, 'I-I-m a bit s-sore."

'We were just talking about you." Seth straightened and chuckled. 'Have you figured out more about your Bentos book?"

All three men looked at me, particularly Caleb. He sat rod straight at his desk, hands spread on the wood with the tips of his fingers white from pressing against it.

'No. I haven't really thought about much since yesterday." *Only yesterday?* It felt like a lifetime ago now.

Caleb slapped a hand down on top of the desk. 'There's word some beasts have headed east. I believe they are either a part of this pack or related somehow." He stared at Michael as if he expected him to say something. Michael didn't.

Seth clapped his hands. 'Enough hunting for one weekend, don't you think Caleb?" He glanced at his watch. 'And I need to get back to my understudy. The Higher Coven will meet again in a few weeks. We can then discuss any new matters that have come to our attention. Take a break, Caleb."

Caleb glowered at Seth. I never knew what the word actually meant, but seeing Caleb's eyes narrow and the anger on his face gave the word more meaning than any dictionary ever could.

'You're going?" I said to Seth. *I'm gonna miss your humor.* It sure worked nicely with the serious one.

'Come and visit anytime... with Michael, of course." He winked and gave a sideways nod in Michael's direction. He turned to Caleb and touched two fingers to his eyebrow in a small salute, then disappeared out of the room before I could even turn my head to follow.

Silence filled the room as all three of us watched the closed door. I inhaled a slow, deep breath and tried to focus my thoughts. What should I ask Caleb? How much do I share? Or how much does he already know? I exhaled and stepped in front of the desk.

Standing in front of his large leather chair, Caleb crossed his arms over his chest. Still a massive figure, it was intimidating to look up. He stared at Michael and then at me, his eyes hiding something behind their blue color. 'Why haven't you been reading your book?"

'Pardon?" He didn't have the decency to ask how I felt? I'd flippin' saved his understudy! He could show me a tidbit amount of respect.

'My concern is that yesterday's outburst may stop you from being able to read the book. We don't want to hinder your gift."

'I'll look when I'm ready," I snapped. 'Why are you so concerned about the book?" A weird sense of protectiveness surrounded my thoughts toward the journal. It was mine, not anyone else's. Especially not his.

He tsked. 'That book could be the key to stopping their race. Make them instinct. Why wouldn't I be anxious?"

Michael shifted beside me and walked over to a case of books. He took the same position Seth had earlier when we'd walked in. A thought crossed my mind. *He's the referee.*

I huffed. 'Is it the book, or me, Caleb? What's got you so pissed?" My heart thundered at the accusation but, somehow, I knew it was right.

Caleb's eyes grew wide then hardened. 'Both," he spat. 'The book for its history. And you... you for your damn ability. You've suddenly become a very important asset." He sighed and dropped into his chair, his facial features softening. 'You're an asset to this family. I-I'm glad Michael took you under his wing."

Michael stepped forward. 'I didn't take her" "

Caleb waved his fingers. 'Irrelevant."

Hands on my hips, I stiffened. 'Whatever you think, Caleb, I don't really care. *That's* irrelevant." I forgot about my body's discomfort. 'There are a few things I want to know. I need to find out about my past. I'm heading back to Niagara Falls. I'm going to find out who I really am." I shot a glance at Michael when he uttered in surprise. This time I held my hand up to stop him from saying anything. 'Damon said the Grollics knew about me when I knew nothing about myself. How can that be?"

Caleb now averted my gaze. 'Sometimes the past should remain buried. Sometimes it is not our right to dig into it."

'Whatever," I snapped, watching Michael's head twist in my direction, his mouth dropping open in surprise. 'Michael's coming with me."

Caleb stiffened. 'He cannot leave now! After what has happened, and the Coven gathering shortly, he cannot be absent."

'I-m going." Michael strode in front of the desk, taking my hand in his. 'You don-t need me here. There is no way I-d let Rouge go on her own."

'Now is not the time to go on a treasure hunt." Caleb glared at me. 'You-re a liability."

'I thought I was an asset." I sighed. Whatever I-d hoped Caleb might know he either wasn-t going to share it with me or simply didn-t know. Fighting him wasn-t going to get me any closer to the truth.

'Have you memorized the book? Are there more words you can command or speak?"

He was never going to let up on the damn journal. 'No. I haven-t touched it since yesterday. Trying to deal with all this crap seems enough on my plate at the moment. I-m not sure if this ability isn-t more of a curse."

Caleb leaned forward, resting his large hands on the desk to get closer. 'It is a gift and you need to develop it. If you truly love Michael, you will see that it-s a way to protect him, to protect all of us."

'Caleb!" Michael warned.

'Michael, please," Caleb said. 'You wanted this girl and brought her here. You had us hunt to save her. This gift is meant to be used *for* us, not against."

Caleb's right. I loved Michael, and if I could protect him in any way, I would do whatever I could. 'I need to find out about my past, and I want to find out about this *thing* I can do." I refused to call it a gift. I had no idea what it was and until I learned more, I somehow didn-t trust it.

'If Rouge wants to go, I-m going with her." Michael pointed a finger at Caleb. 'If she wanted to study the Grollic book, there will be no pushing from you or the Coven. She is *not* one of us. We give her the freedom to do as she pleases. No pressure. I will not allow her to be used as a pawn for your games." He gently pulled my fingers, still interlaced in his hand toward him.

Without another word, we walked out of the office. Michael nodded at Grace as we walked by her in the living room, continuing through the kitchen and out the door to the cottage. We walked in silence till we got inside the pool house. I never thought about one ounce of pain as we moved.

Michael closed the door and stood inches from me. 'I-m so sorry I spoke for you, but I cannot let you become a pawn in Caleb-s games. I know he-s already making plans to use you, and I refuse to let that happen. The Coven would jump at his suggestions if he tells them of the potential power you have. I promise you, I will not let that happen. We will leave before I allow that. No matter what I agreed to before I met you."

Before? I pushed the question out of my mind and put my hand on his warm cheek. 'You can-t run from what you have spent a lifetime building. You were part of this Coven, long before you knew me."

Michael rested his head on the wall and sighed. 'Let-s travel that road when, or if, we ever reach it." He chewed his lip for a moment, and then straightened. 'I still have a birthday present to give you."

I-d completely forgotten.

'Go sit on the futon." Michael walked over to the stand on the side I slept on and opened the top drawer. He came around and kneeled down so we were almost at the same height. He held his hand palm up towards me. On his hand rested a very pretty, small, sparkly, garnet-red wrapped rectangular box.

I looked at his face to see if it would give anything away. His expression betrayed nothing, even his eyes remained a cool blue. With both hands, I gently lifted the box from his and lifted the lid. A small chain slid to the side. I glanced up.

His eyes darted from my hands to my eyes and back down again. Worry created small lines between his eyebrows. Dropping my gaze, the inside of the box stole my breath away.

Inside laid his Siorghra on the black velvet. The beautiful Celtic silver design glistened off the red inside it. Slowly and with shaking hands, I removed it from the box and, without saying a word, held it out to him. I turned and lifted my hair out of the way so he could put it around my neck.

From the mirror s reflection I saw the doubt he d had the moment before was gone, replaced with a tender smile. His eyes changed to a lighter shade of blue, and he leaned forward to hang the necklace around my neck.

With a sexy, throaty laugh, he said, ' I d be honored if you would wear my Siorghra. I love you. I would do anything for you – fight for you, follow you, travel across this world for you, do anything you ask. I d die for you. This is my love, eternally." He looped the clasp together and a resounding click echoed in my ears. I loved the sound.

' You have my heart forever." I shifted so I could put my hands on his face to bring it towards me.

We kissed gently, and I could feel him holding back, afraid he might hurt me. I pushed my lips harder against his and pressed against him. He made me feel safe.

He lifted his lips away from mine as he looked into my eyes. I could see his were a darker shade of blue, and I was sure mine were full of desire as well. His lips came crashing down on mine and both of us felt each other's desire.

The cuts on my lip broke open and I could taste blood in my mouth. Michael jumped off me onto his back. I gingerly rolled over to my side and pressed my wrist to my lip to stop the bleeding."

He gave a small smile and brushed a stray hair from my forehead. ' I m sorry. Are you okay? I didn t realize the effect of putting my Siorghra around your neck would have on me."

I leaned up on one elbow and smiled. 'I-m fine. You know something really cool? It-s-like I can feel the change, too." I didn-t- feel alone. I felt connected. ' It-s-the best feeling in the world."

We grinned, staring at each other like a couple of school kids.

A thought crossed my mind. ' How did you know where to find me when Damon took me?"

Michael sat up and leaned against the frame of the futon. He lifted me so my head could rest against his lap.

' I wasn-t-sure where you were, but I knew you were alive. I-m not sure how I knew, I just did. As the Coven meeting finished, Grace messaged me that you hadn-t- returned from grocery shopping. Caleb, Seth, and I left immediately. I couldn-t-get back here fast enough.

' We searched the grocery stores, your old house, out by the school, out by where the bonfire night had been this summer. Nothing gave us your scent. The falling snow slowed us, making it harder to catch it and I started to grow desperate. We searched all night." He paused, as if to collect his thoughts. ' I thought Damon had taken you to get to me. It never really occurred to Seth, Caleb, or I that he might actually want you and our deaths might just be a bonus. It all makes more sense now."

' How-d- you know where to look?" I played with the pendant around my neck, loving the feeling of the loop running along the chain.

"Sarah located the GPS tracking on the Jeep and figured a way into the car dealership-s-computer. We found the Jeep towards the early morning, and I found my *Siorghra* under the seat."

I nodded. After seeing the connection between Seth and Tatiana, I-d-hoped he-d-had some inner connection to the pendant.

' Seth went into the cabin and I raced into the forest. Caleb followed me and we both found the empty cabin. I followed the trail of blood that led around the lake. I knew it was yours, I could smell the black liquorice scent. Caleb took off in another direction.

I came to the spot where you must have stopped for a moment. One of those mongrels was tearing some of your clothes. It was a trap. The pack had hid and used the one Grollic to pretend it was mauling you." Michael shuddered and lightly made trails with his fingers on my back. When he stopped, a finger rested on the birthmark he hadn-t seen.

I moved slightly, nervous he might know about the mark and wanted me to tell him about it. I planned to, just not until I figured everything out.

The mark seemed to hold something which could tear us apart. I wasn-t ready for that. We-d only just found each other. I touched his arm and his fingers began tracing light circles absently on my shoulder. 'What happened next?" I asked.

'I over-reacted, and I never do that." He shook his head. 'Enraged I attacked and, stupid me, was instantly surrounded by the pack. Caleb took off after the Alpha. The rest you pretty much know as it was a few moments later that I saw you come back from the lake. You looked so fragile and scared. However, that changed when you started hollering at the Grollics. You were pretty pissed off."

I smiled, remembering my anger and how stupid a mistake it could have turned out to have been. I thought about the journal. When I studied it again, I-d see it in a whole new light. 'Do you think more Grollics are going to come after me?"

Michael ran his fingers along the side of my ribcage, staying quiet for a long time. 'Eventually I think they will. We don-t know how many of them know about you or if they know you are able to command them. I think, to them, you are bigger than our war."

Thanks goodness we were laying close together. I needed his warmth because the words he spoke made my blood run cold and my birthmark began to burn with a sharp pain I-d never felt before.

POSTLUDE

NOTE TO SELF

Remember to keep writing in this notebook, Rouge. You bought this silly, expensive leather notebook to keep track of your thoughts for your trip this summer. You also promised yourself that you were going to write down anything you learned from the Grollic book. So, this is your journal and, one day, you are going to want to sit down and read this book to remember all the emotions and things you learned on this journey.

I sat tapping the pen against the desk while I tried to think of what else to write on the first page.

Rouge, you love Michael with every part of your being. This is something bigger than just you here. It is in the blood which runs through you. Don't ever forget that or lose sight of it – no matter what happens in the future. Always remember - you need him forever.

I thought about the mark on my back and leaned forward, forcing the image out of my mind.

One other important thing – A GROLLIC IS THE ENEMY (...I think)

THE END

Book 3

Coming 2014

Hidden Secrets Saga:
Download Seventh Mark part 1 For FREE
Book Trailer:
http://www.youtube.com/watch?v=Y-_vVYC1gvo

ldhbfd

B 4

Book Blurb:

Like most teenagers, Rouge is trying to figure out who she is and what she wants to be. With little knowledge about her past, she has questions but has never tried to find the answers. Everything changes when she befriends a strangely intoxicating family. Siblings Grace and Michael, appear to have secrets which seem connected to Rouge. Her hunch is confirmed when a horrible incident occurs at an outdoor party. Rouge may be the only one who can find the answer.

An ancient journal, a Sioghra necklace and a special mark force life-altering decisions for a girl who grew up unprepared to fight for her life or others.

All secrets have a cost and Rouge's determination to find the truth can only lead to trouble...or something even more sinister.

Shadow of Doubt
Part 1 is FREE!
Book Trailer: http://www.youtube.com/watch?v=LZK09Fe7kgA

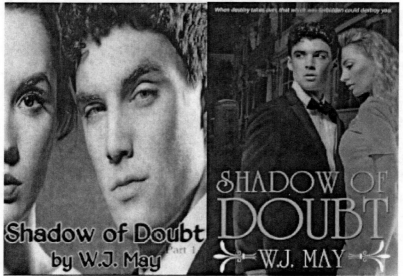

Book Blurb:

What happens when you fall for the one you are forbidden to love?

Erebus is a bit of a lost soul. He's a guy so he should be out to have fun but unlike the rest of his kind, he is solemn and withdrawn. That is, until he meets Aurora, a law student at Cornell University. His entire world is shaken. Feelings he's never had and urges he's never understood take over. These strange longings drive him to question everything about himself.

When a jealous ex stalks back into his life, he must decide if he is willing to risk everything to be with Aurora. His desire for her could destroy her, or worse, erase his own existence forever.

Read the next installment of:
THE CHRONICLES OF KERRIGAN

Rae of Hope is FREE!
Book Trailer:
http://www.youtube.com/watch?v=gILAwXxx8MU

BOOK BLURB:

How hard do you have to shake the family tree to find the truth about the past?

Fifteen year-old Rae Kerrigan never really knew her family's history. Her mother and father died when she was young and it is only when she accepts a scholarship to the prestigious Guilder Boarding School in England that a mysterious family secret is revealed.

Will the sins of the father be the sins of the daughter?

As Rae struggles with new friends, a new school and a star-struck forbidden love, she must also face the ultimate challenge: receive a tattoo on her sixteenth birthday with specific powers that may bind her to an unspeakable darkness. It's up to Rae to undo the dark evil in her family's past and have a ray of hope for her future.

Free Books:

COMING SOON:

Book Blurb:

What if courage was your only option?

When Kallie lands a college interview with the city's new hot-shot police officer, she has no idea everything in her life is about to change. The detective is young, handsome and seems to have an unnatural ability to stop the increasing local crime rate. Detective Liam's particular interest in Kallie sends her heart and head stumbling over each other.

When a raging blood feud between vampires spills into her home, Kallie gets caught in the middle. Torn between love and family loyalty she must find the courage to fight what she fears the most and possibly risk everything, even if it means dying for those she loves.

Did you love *Seventh Mark - Part 2*? Then you should read *Rae of Hope* by W.J. May!

How hard do you have to shake the family tree to find the truth about the past?

Fifteen year-old Rae Kerrigan never really knew her family's history. Her mother and father died when she was young and it is only when she accepts a scholarship to the prestigious Guilder Boarding School in England that a mysterious family secret is revealed.

Will the sins of the father be the sins of the daugther?

As Rae struggles with new friends, a new school and a star-struck forbidden love, she must also face the ultimate challenge: receive a tattoo on her sixteenth birthday with specific powers that may bind her to an unspeakable darkness. It's up to Rae to undo the dark evil in her family's past and have a ray of hope for her future.

Also by W.J. May

Hidden Secrets Saga
Seventh Mark - Part 1
Seventh Mark - Part 2

The Chronicles of Kerrigan
Rae of Hope
Dark Nebula
House of Cards

The Hidden Secrets Saga
Seventh Mark (part 1 & 2)

The Senseless Series
Radium Halos
Radium Halos - Part 2

Standalone
Shadow of Doubt (Part 1 & 2)
Five Shades of Fantasy
Glow - A Young Adult Fantasy Sampler

Shadow of Doubt - Part 1
Shadow of Doubt - Part 2
Four and a Half Shades of Fantasy
Full Moon
Dream Fighter

CPSIA information can be obtained at www.ICGtesting.com
Printed in the USA
LVOW11s1403050715

445015LV00006B/53/P